FOREVER
IN THESE
PAGES

…some love stories last only in books

FOREVER IN THESE PAGES

...some love stories last only in books

Meghna

Srishti
PUBLISHERS & DISTRIBUTORS

Srishti Publishers & Distributors
N-16, C. R. Park
New Delhi 110 019
editorial@srishtipublishers.com

First published by
Srishti Publishers & Distributors in 2013

Copyright © Meghna, 2013

10 9 8 7 6 5 4 3 2

Typeset by EGP at Srishti

This is where our story begins, where your path meets mine ...
and no matter where this road may lead you tomorrow,
our journey will be one filled with love.
It may not last forever, but some of the best love stories don't.
— Meghna

To the one without whom this book would not be possible,
To all my friends who have always believed in me,
And to all reading this right now to remind you to always believe in love!

KINGDOM OF LOVE

B eing in love is one of the most beautiful experiences ever. Not only does one celebrate love as the most ecstatic state of being, love also has more power than anything else in the world. While it completes some who are lucky enough to be loved in return, it also in one moment can destroy some others when they lose someone they love and are left with a deep emptiness within their hearts.

Love is not just an emotion or feeling; it is an experience in itself. Whether good or bad, it is this experience that makes us all define love in our own various ways.

We have all grown up on stories of love from fairy tales that our parents read to us; where the prince always found his princess at the end of difficult ordeals and they lived happily ever after. And then there are movies where the girl realizes she is in love with her best friend who was there all along and she just didn't realize it until he started falling for someone else. Or the guy who initially does not see the girl's love for him and then when she leaves him, chases her across the country to win her back.

It is one emotion most written about, most talked of, heard of, and even experienced. We all at some point have fallen - in love, or out of it. Yet it's a word that can never truly be explained, as one import will never hold true for more than a few people.

Thomas Middleton, an English dramatist (1570-1626), attempted to define love in a way, I think, everyone would relate to; or at least I do.

"*Love is all in fire, and yet is ever freezing. Love is much in winning, yet is more in losing. Love is ever sick, and yet is never dying. Love is ever true, and yet is ever lying. Love does dote in liking and is mad in loathing. Love indeed is everything, yet indeed is nothing."*

Love does not acknowledge bars of age, caste or society and the depth of feelings runs to the very core of our being the first time we feel it. Everyone remembers the first time they fell in love and some of us are lucky enough to have that first love last forever. Then there are others who spend the rest of their lives looking for that kind of love again.

But where does one find such love again? It's difficult to find love in a world where trust is like a thin sheet of ice, threatening to break any second and feelings don't run deep and people only show what others want to see.

When you give someone too much love, they tend to take you for granted. When what you give is not enough, they look for it with others and chase it. It's all just one big exhausting game.

The problem is love is as simple in theory as relationships are complicated in reality. Relationships will never be simple; you will rarely walk into true love with ease and be successful in holding on to it. You could bump into the right person at the wrong time; or end up being with the wrong person when the time is right. And at times, you realize your love with someone right after that person walks out of your life.

In real life, the prince doesn't always recognize his princess, and the knight in shining armour, whoever said all that glitters is not gold, was super accurate. We love those who don't love us in return, a term commonly known as unrequited love, which is the worst kind of love. Then there are those people whom we meet who are completely in love with us but we don't feel the same. In reality relationships can be defined in one word 'complicated.'

All this aside, there are three things I have learnt about love through my own experience. Firstly, love is something that you will find when you least expect it. It's sneaky and tends to creep up behind you when you're not looking.

Secondly, the good ones are not all taken. There is still someone waiting for you and it is only when you meet the perfect person that you will wonder why they are not taken yet!

Thirdly, some of the best love stories don't necessarily have a happy ending. Haven't we all heard of 'Romeo and Juliet'?

I am Aleah, and this is my story.

I WISHED ON EVERY STAR THAT FELL

Just like any other young girl, I spent a fair amount of time reading fairy tales. I firmly believed in true love, charming princes, and love stories ending with happily ever afters'. And then, I grew up. As I embraced being a teenager, my belief in love strengthened, thanks to all the love stories I read and watched. I watched one romantic movie after another, imaging myself in place of every actress and knowing that one of those stories would turn true for me and my prince too. The many Mills & Boon books I read a few years later only reconfirmed my belief: there were romantic, ideal, loving men like those in the pages out *there* and one of them was just for me. However, '*there*' was a place I was yet to find.

No wonder I earned myself the title of a 'hopeless romantic' among all my friends. The way they rolled their eyes every time I talked about love or finding my perfect guy made their eyeballs take a tour around the earth.

I always hoped I would find that perfect guy. I did meet a lot of guys, but almost all of them always fell short of my image of *the* guy. I never felt that special moment where you know this is it; that inevitable spark, with any of those guys. I guess I just couldn't find someone who could make me fall in love with them the way I always imagined.

After awhile, the magic, as if, vanished and took the special moments, sparks, and tingly feeling or butterflies in the stomach along with it. As I realised the increasing absence of these special feelings, I did something that all of us do at some point of time in our lives: I embraced reality. I locked up those so-called silly childhood dreams, and hid them somewhere deep in a corner of my heart. They say you shouldn't settle for anything less than butterflies; but for me, consolation became the new love and love became complicated.

Then one fine day, I did meet a boy. His name was Jeremy. The boy I had met in Bombay when I was completing my MBA. When one of my classmates introduced me to him, we realised that we got along well. I enjoyed our conversations which were always so witty; they kept me on my toes.

Jeremy was like the handsome stranger one reads about in *Jane Austen* books. He was tall and handsome, the kind of man you could take home to your mother. He would make the perfect husband. Unfortunately, I met him only a month before my course was over and had to fly back home to Dubai soon after. So we continued our friendship over long distance.

It was only some months later when I flew back to Bombay for my convocation that we entered into an unstated relationship. I was disheartened that I would have to go all the way back to Dubai just when things had started working out.

But luck was on my side and I got a job in Delhi and lived with my sister, who was completing her graduation in the same city. It was a moment she had been waiting for and it worked out perfectly for me as it got me a little closer to Jeremy.

We stayed in touch constantly and made it a point to talk to each other almost every day. He would often fly down and surprise me. However, it had now been almost eight months I had last seen him. Between the two of us, neither of us was managing to get time to see each other until finally he managed to get a day's leave and took the first flight out straight to me. I could not wait to see him.

ONCE UPON A COLD EVENING

Rocking to the rock music at one of my favourite places in the city, I was enjoying the continuous flow of alcohol, and the decent crowd. Well the crowd did not really matter. I was at one of my favourite places, with my closest bunch of friends, and Jeremy had flown in just for a day. It was perfect!

Jeremy and I had just gotten our drinks when Rohan walked in. This was the second time I was seeing Rohan; my friend Karan had introduced me to him before and we had totally hit it off. I was really looking forward to see him again and hoping he would come.

The first time I met Rohan. It was a surreal night. Rohan had dropped me home and the bottle of gold tequila in his car was utilised well. We had bonded over tequila and chatted like we had been friends for a long time. There was something different about Rohan. The way he looked at me, this intense gaze, it felt like I might fall completely and uncontrollably in love with him if I looked into his eyes for too long. Ok, maybe I'm exaggerating a little but it did make me feel a little uncomfortable, yet it felt completely normal.

As I recovered from these thoughts, we got a table and sat down. The seating plan was clear in my mind; I thought Jeremy would come and sit right beside me. But he just stood there, and instead, Rohan came and took the seat next to me. I was disappointed with Jeremy at his lack of interest in wanting to spend time with me. On the other hand something about Rohan made my heart skip a beat. And I was just a little afraid that Jeremy would feel the slight tension between me and Rohan.

I tried to divert my mind by taking all my attention back to

Jeremy. I could barely hear him over the loud music and could see him straining to hear me. I tried to make conversation with him but eventually he just choose to speak to my friends sitting next to him and I started chatting with Rohan. After talking to him about general things for a while, I slowly leant in, and quietly whispered, "Do you still have tequila?"

"It's in the car. Do you want to go have some?"

"Yes, we can all go and have some?"

"There isn't much this time…"

"Only the two of us will go then, we won't share," I said, after thinking about it for a moment.

His face lit up and he laughed, "So you're sure you don't mind that we just leave Jeremy here?"

I was stung by a sudden jolt of guilt; I didn't want him to see that so quickly covered up, saying, "Well no! I am not planning to leave him or anything. We will go for a bit and since you're going to drop us back, I will leave these shopping bags in the car, have a few sips, and come back quickly?"

He was trying hard to hide his smile and readily agreed with a quick "Okay".

We both got up. I told Jeremy I was going to keep the bags in Rohan's car and would come back in a few minutes. He didn't really seem to care and just gave me this approving nod. I expected, and actually wanted Jeremy to be a little jealous of my going away with Rohan even if it was just to keep bags in a car, and his lack of any such emotion bothered me.

When Rohan and I reached the car, he asked me what was wrong.

I was surprised that he had realised something was bothering me, especially since I was trying so hard to hide it. I was not sure of sharing my thoughts with him yet. "Nothing much; relationships are just complicated," I said, trying to fake a smile.

He smiled back at me and didn't say anything. After a long pause he dug the bottle of tequila out and broke the silence, "sip?" I smiled. We talked for a while as we took sips and passed the tequila bottle back and forth. I finally told him I was upset. He was easy to talk to. It felt like I had known him for a long while; maybe from a past life. I had this strange feeling in the pit of my stomach, and it was not a familiar feeling. It was not butterflies for sure, and I was not uneasy too. It was a pleasant and rather comfortable feeling, which brought an involuntary smile to my face every now and then. It scared me a little to feel like this, and that too for Rohan while Jeremy waited for me in there. It could not be real. I felt a teeny bit guilty for enjoying his company and the ease of our conversations and soon told Rohan it was time to head back.

When we went back inside, I decided to stop analyzing this connection that seemed to exist between me and Rohan. It wasn't some crazy attraction or love at first sight but he made me laugh.

I enjoyed the rest of the night. With nice music filling the air around me, I stood up to dance with my friends. I looked over at Jeremy a few times thinking he would get the hint and join me but he didn't budge. I finally went up to him and asked him to dance with me; he was reluctant and wanted to have another drink. So, he refused and just went to the bar for a refill. I knew he was not much of a dancer but didn't understand if he came to spend time with me or to drink.

I don't know if it was the dancing, or the atmosphere, or Jeremy's lack of interest in me, but in due course of the night, I somehow ended up in Rohan's arms. He held me close but not too close, as if that's exactly where he wanted me to be. I began to feel a teeny bit guilty and soon enough he gave me this knowing look like he understood and we kept our distance. The rest of the night I stayed by Jeremy's side and avoided Rohan, till it was time to leave.

Outside, in the parking lot, there was a cold wind blowing. I was covered in goose bumps and was ready to freeze any moment. I turned towards Jeremy and said, "It's freezing out here." My heart half wished him to be romantic and put his arm around me. But nothing of that sort happened; so much for romance.

He just looked back at me with a blank look and said, "It *is* damn cold."

Rohan could overhear us as we were walking together; after a brief moment he asked me if I was feeling cold, even though he already knew the answer to that.

"Very," I responded sadly and with slight annoyance, all the while trying to keep a smile on my face.

"I have my hoodie in the car. Do you want it?"

"Yes please, thank you" I said as we all walked towards his car to get it.

I made a mental note of this chivalry and realised that I liked that quality in a man. The hoodie was a bit too big for me and I could have comfortably had another me in there, but it was warm. It had his scent, strong and masculine. Every breath felt like he was standing right there.

It was very late when we finally left for home. Rohan drove me and Jeremy home. There was an awkward silence in the car as Rohan drove, Jeremy stared out of the window and I kept wondering why ever since Jeremy got here he seemed so uninterested.

While in the car, sitting on the back seat, there was this one moment, I know for sure, I will remember as long as I live. I was sitting behind Rohan and I could see him in the rear view mirror. And then I suddenly found Rohan looking right back at me. It wasn't exactly a stare; it was more like we locked gazes with each other and neither of us took our eyes away from each other. My heart was beating so fast, I thought it'd race out of my body. It lasted a brief moment but I will never forget the way he looked at me.

When we reached home, Jeremy walked out of the car saying a vague goodbye to Rohan. I got out of the car and saw that Jeremy had already reached half way towards the door. I quickly thanked Rohan. He smiled, waved his hand slightly and drove off.

As we entered into my house, I realized I still had Rohan's hoodie on. I took it off and placed it carefully on the chair as I smiled to myself.

I was too afraid to feel the way I did. When I closed my eyes, I remembered his intense gaze. When he looked at me, I felt as if he could see past all my masks and defences. It seemed he could see every secret I have ever kept, every fear I that haunted me, and every disappointment I have ever felt. I wasn't used to feeling like this. It left like a scene from a movie.

As I was enmeshed in my thoughts, just then, reality kicked in. Jeremy had to leave soon; his cab had almost arrived. He had flown in for just one day and now was the time for him to go back. I asked him if he needed something before he left and suggested a light coffee to keep him warm. He readily agreed and offered to help me make it

We were sitting at the dinning table with two steaming cups of coffee when he got all romantic, all of a sudden. He started telling me all the things he liked about me. I didn't interrupt him or ask him the reasons for this sudden change. I just listened to his words as they warmed my heart.

I looked up at him when he stopped speaking and told him, "I will miss you. I wish you didn't have to go and could have stayed longer."

"I will see you soon. You said you might be coming to Mumbai, right?"

"Yes."

His phone rang before I could say anything else. It was the cabbie informing him of the cab's arrival.

"My cab's here now, I have to go."

I walked him to the door. He kissed me on my forehead and told me he loved me.

"What did you say?" I asked him for I was not sure he had just said it.

"You heard what I said." His smile was sincere.

I was a little surprised at this. In the one-and-a-half years that I had been with him, this was the first time Jeremy had told me he loved me.

"I know. I'm just making sure I heard the right thing. Are you sure? Well, and the question is, can you say it again?"

He held my hand in between both of his and looked right into my eyes saying, "I love you, Ali. I love you, I love you, and I love you. Is that enough or do you want me to say it again?"

He wore a Mona Lisa smile and I laughed, "It's good enough for now. And I love you, too."

He put his arms around me and hugged me. It was followed by a quick goodbye kiss.

"I have to go now," he said as he slowly moved away and reached out for his suitcase.

"Bye," I said feeling a little sad.

"Bye. Take care of yourself, oaky!"

"I will."

With that, he sat in the cab and went off. I was left with a big bag of tumultuous feelings. I had no idea what was happening; way too many things simultaneously.

IRONY CALLED LIFE

I had just woken up, and was still very lazy to get out of bed. I lay there, staring at the ceiling reminiscing about the events of the previous night. I laughed at myself for being so stupid. I was behaving like a teenager. This wasn't a movie or some frivolous game; it was real life. I was sure moments like these don't last for too long, and this one would pass soon.

I was lost in thought and was desperately trying to rationalize what was going on around me. Just then, I got startled by the sound of my phone ringing, the new Keisha song blaring loudly. It was Laksh calling.

I smiled when I saw his name flashing on the phone screen because he was the one person who knew everything about me. For a guy, he made a really good agony aunt and had been there for me whenever I felt completely lost. I could always depend on him to help me figure out my feelings or thoughts. He was always honest, and would say things as they were. It helps to have someone act as a constant reality check and to keep telling me to not deny how I really felt.

The moment I answered the phone, I blurted out, "Something happened last night". I had missed the hello and as I finished saying this one sentence, I could feel my heart skip a beat.

"What happened?" Laksh asked laughing.

"Don't laugh! Well, it's a good thing. Like it-can't-be-true kind of good. Jeremy told me he loves me. Wait let me tell you everything from the beginning. I met this guy. I mean I met him before and met him again yesterday. You know Karan, right? The friend I told you about. He introduced me to Rohan. We were all out, chilling yesterday and Jeremy was also here. But, you know what! Rohan had dropped me home the night we met first, and we totally hit it off. There was this moment where he looked at me. Okay so, I can't really explain it, but he looked at me with this intense gaze. Usually that kind of stuff is creepy, but it didn't feel creepy the way he did. You know what I mean, right?

"It made a little nervous. It was like a fluttery feeling in the pit of my stomach. I am not supposed to feel the fluttering and all this paraphernalia. This doesn't happen; not to me at least. It's not real, it can't be."

Laksh seemed to be suppressing his laughter at my behaving like a teenager, I presumed. But I ignored it and I continued with what I was saying.

"Oh, and anyway, then last night I met him again. We spent some quality time together; we talked and we even danced a little. He is so easy to talk to, like I'm not my usual 'why should I tell you' self with him. I loved just talking to him and getting to know him and really enjoyed his company. What's wrong with me? I have Jeremy. For almost two years, I have wanted to be with Jeremy. I know Jeremy and I have been in a complicated sort of relationship, but I have put in so much into it. To top it all up, he told me he loved me last night, he stood there and looked at me in the eyes and told me he loves me. I can't just ignore it."

I had said it all in one go and there was a pregnant pause when I finished saying all that. It was only after a few seconds that Laksh finally spoke.

"Aleah, relax! There is nothing wrong with you; you just need to breathe. You are thinking too much about everything and over analyzing the situation as always creating unnecessary trouble and confusion for your brain. I am sure it was just one of those moments which happen and then it's forgotten. Just let it be for a while and don't over analyse it. Nobody is asking you to leave Jeremy or anything. Oh and what's with the dancing and all? Where was Jeremy when this entire Rohan thing was happening? And let me just get this straight… Jeremy told you he loved you?" Laksh sounded as surprised by the Jeremy bit as I had imagined him to be. He never disappointed me.

I was smiling as I told Laksh what had happened. "Jeremy was also there but was being all aloof. He kept hanging at the bar as if he had come to Delhi for a day to drink. And you know what, this is the first time in all this time that I have been with Jeremy or in almost eight years for that matter that someone has made me feel like this It's insane, that too when Jeremy finally admits how he feels about me and tells me he loves me. Though I don't understand how he could be so aloof and still say he loves me. How fucked up is that!"

Laksh's voice was serious now. "I know you have put a lot of effort into your relationship with Jeremy and it finally seems to be working out. Think about Jeremy; let the Rohan thing be the way it is for now it could just be a moment. Get to know Rohan more be friends with him, there is nothing wrong with that and if you still feel there is something more to it, figure it out then."

"You are right. I should just be friends with Rohan and not think so much. I don't know why I'm making such a big deal about it, I think I watch to many romantic movies," I said calmly, feeling a little better like I was in control of the situation again.

"All girls do. Are you meeting Rohan anytime again soon?" Laksh asked.

My heart skipped a beat at the thought of meeting him again. I ignored it.

"No plans yet, will keep you posted."

"Okay then! Call me whenever."

The phone call ended with that, but I stayed in bed thinking about it. I had met Jeremy about two years ago and it had taken a while for me to get really close to him. He was mature and responsible, exactly the type of person you would want to be with when you're in your mid-twenties.

I took a trip down memory lane and tried to search for my definition of love. That's when I realised that experience had taught me that true love belongs in movies and books, not real life. Jeremy was a mature person, maybe not romantic, but we both believed that being practical in matters of the heart really works.

He didn't give me butterflies or make my heart skip a beat every now and then, but he was there when I needed him. That's how it works in real life. The teenage dream of finding a guy whose world revolves around you was bullshit and I had come to understand it well.

I knew I needed to talk to Jeremy about the way I felt and his stand offish behaviour. I just had no idea when to bring it up. Laksh was right I couldn't let one moment define my life. Maybe I was just reading too much into it.

NO PROMISES

Since lying in bed wasn't going to solve anything, I got up and went to the kitchen to find something to eat. I had just about finished my breakfast when I heard the faint sound of my phone ringing. I ran to my room and found it buried under my pillow. It was Jeremy calling.

"Hello," I said as I started walking towards the balcony.

"Did I wake you?" He asked, knowing how I loved waking up late on weekends.

"No," I replied, smiling at the thought that he knew me so well. "I have already finished breakfast and everything."

He laughed, "I reached safely, thought I would let you know."

I said, "Okay, hope you are not too tired with all that travelling."

He spoke softly, "I am not. Which reminds me, I hope you had a nice time last night?"

I laughed, "I hope you didn't get too bored hanging out with my friends."

"They were nice. What was that guy's name who dropped us I forgot to thank him?"

"Rohan."

"Rohan," he said, in a tone I did not care for much.

"Yes."

"I noticed you both seemed to be getting along quiet well," he said, slyly masking his question within a statement. He often did that; spoke in riddles. It was difficult having a straight forward conversation with him. He always spoke in riddles.

"We are friends."

"I know."

"Then why this whole 'Rohan' thing?" I asked. "A few hours ago you told me you love me. I thought that meant something for us." I could read the annoyance in my own voice as I walked back into the house.

"I do." I was just asking Ali. I said what I really meant to say" His voice had softened instantly.

"Can I also ask you something?" I wanted to be very sure of things between us. "What does this mean Jeremy? You said you love me, but are you still planning to date other people?"

"Where did that come from?"

"That's the way it's been hasn't it. Even though we have been together because of the distance or whatever it is you haven't really committed to me and I want to know what you telling me you love me really means to you?"

"It's not like I'm going and looking for people, Ali. It's just that I'm still not making any promises."

After being with him for almost two years and after his profession of love a few hours back, it felt like it always had, like nothing changed, like those three words were just words. I still did not know what he meant; he always confused me with his hot and cold behavior.

They say, actions speak louder than words. But with him, it was not the case at all. He himself used to keep saying that to me and now his words and action didn't match. He behaved as if he wanted all the same things I did when we were together, but in the end he would always never really commit. It frustrated me and left me stranded in no man's land, literally as much as figuratively. I was in no mood to get into an argument so early in the day and changed the topic. I had a light-hearted conversation for the next five minutes before we hung up. I still could not understand what he wanted.

I decided to stop thinking about it and go have a relaxing shower.

The heat of the water steamed up the bathroom so much that

I could not see anything. Droplets of hot water fell with force against my body and rolled off. I let them wash away all my thoughts of Jeremy. He may have said he still wanted to see other people or in his words not make any promises, but he told me he loves me and the one thing I was sure about was that he meant it. Even though at this moment it felt like mere words, but the fact that he had said it was enough to make me stay put until we figured things out.

When I got out of the shower I noticed I had a message from Rohan.

"So when do I get my hoodie back?"

I laughed as my fingers typed out the words, "And what if I want to keep it?"

About five minutes, the phone buzzed with his reply, "You can if you want to, but when do I see you next?"

I realized how the thought of seeing him again always made me smile. I liked him. But it made me miss Jeremy. I wished it was him that was making me smile but Jeremy just confused me. The fact of the matter was that I wanted to be with him and had given it all I could in the past two years. All I was waiting for was for Jeremy to be sure that he wanted to be with me. But somehow even despite his I love you he didn't want to commit.

I WOULD NEVER SHARE YOU

A few days later, I met Rohan for an evening drive and dinner It was a chilly evening and the breeze gave me goose bumps all over my arms as I waited at the main gate of my house for him to pick me up. I was nervous at the prospect of seeing him. I could feel my heart race as his car slowed down and stopped right in front of me. I got into the car and greeted him cheerfully.

It was warm inside the car as against the nip outside. My goose bumps disappeared in no time. I looked over at him sitting there in the driver's seat. He was always calm, as if nothing in the world could bother him. He turned to look at me with that same intense look I had noticed earlier. I could feel my cheeks burning and turning red. I quickly turned my attention to the road but could sense his smile from the corner of my eye.

"What are you thinking?" He asked.

"Just wondering where we are headed" I said, trying to control my heart which was beating so fast I would not be surprised if he could hear it.

"Where do you want to go?" He asked looking at me again.

I pretended not to notice him looking at me, as I answered his question. "Anywhere, I thought we could grab a bite somewhere, maybe a coffee shop or just go somewhere for dinner."

"Dinner sounds good. How about Big Chill or something? "

"Yes sure," I said smiling.

This was followed by a silent and short drive and soon enough we were there. As he pulled into the parking lot of, he turned towards me and smiled. I smiled back thinking he might just turn out to be my new best friend.

After we sat down on in the most comfortable place we find and ordered our food.   We started talking about almost everything. We spoke about our past, present, and ourselves. It was kind of... I don't know the correct word, but I would say surreal. We were comfortable talking to each other and I didn't feel the need to hide anything from him. I don't know if it was instincts or just some divine intervention, but this just felt right.

We talked about who we were; what we wanted to be in an existential sense, we even talked about our families and likes and dislikes. We realized we had quite a few things in common. I began to realize what it was about him that I liked. He was open to talk about the way he felt about things whether it was family or friends or anything. I could relate to that. That was one thing that was lacking in my relationship with Jeremy. Jeremy was emotionally closed he wouldn't talk about how he felt. He did tell me about things personal to him and how he felt but it was always like a general fact than an emotion.

After about an hour-and-a-half of getting to know each other, I drifted off into my world of day dreams, like I so often did. I had noticed a cute habit in Rohan; he felt annoyed when he didn't know what I was thinking about and he almost always made it a point to ask me as if I was just not allowed to keep any secrets from him. I liked the fact that he cared enough to notice and wanted to know and put that effort in to get to know me. I smiled as he said, "You know you can tell me anything, right?"

"I was just thinking about my whole situation with Jeremy. It's just kind of messed up and confusing." He knew that I was seeing Jeremy and that we'd been together for quite a while; but I had not told him the entire story.

"Why is it messed up?" He asked as he leaned back turning his complete attention towards me.

"I want to be with him, but it's just not happening" I said, trying to hide the frustration and sadness in my voice.

"If that's what you want, then make it happen," his tone was serious, yet affectionate.

"The thing is I want a person who would want me back the

same way as I want him. I want someone who realizes my value in his life, and who wants to be with me and not let me go. Jeremy doesn't seem to be doing that. I don't understand why he wants to see other girls or why he cannot promise me that he won't see anyone else and just be mine? He just doesn't want to commit and yet he tells me he loves me what sense does that make. What is his problem? Am I not good enough? He should care! He should want me to be his and nobody else's! Is that too much to ask for? Wouldn't you want to be with someone who doesn't want to ever lose you?" I said looking at him, somehow hoping he would put me out of my misery.

He did not take his eyes off my face as he moved a little closer, held my hand, and said, "How can you even say you're not good enough. If I was with you, I would never share you."

I didn't know if he was just saying that to make me feel better but in that moment, all I could think of was, I wish he was with me. I don't know why I thought that. He was asking me to fix things with Jeremy and give it my best shot. I could not help but wonder how he knew just what to say. He interrupted my thoughts and said, "For me, either I am completely with someone, or I'm not." Every word he said seemed so sweet to my ears. What would I not give to have Jeremy feel that way for me. Rohan was right! If you're with someone and you love them, you won't want to see other people. It made me wonder what was wrong with me; I wanted to be with someone who didn't seem to value me. After a brief moment of silence he asked, "What are you thinking?"

I smiled as I said, "I don't like sharing either. I don't want to share the person I'm with, with other people" I could feel my cheeks turn red as I finished the sentence.

"Then why don't you talk to him and fix it, and tell him what you want."

I looked at him, trying to read him. I wanted to understand him. What was it about him that made it so easy being around him? It felt so natural; it was so comforting, like nothing in the world could upset me.

"Again you are thinking! What's wrong?" He said with mock anger, a smile twinkling in his eyes.

I laughed, "I was thinking that maybe I should talk to him and work things out."

"You should. That's what you want, isn't it?" He said looking at me, without blinking.

I responded with a nod. Since I was not quite sure what I really wanted, all I knew was that it was the practical thing to do at that moment.

We continued to talk, he told me about his past relationships and heartbreaks. We got each other and understood where the other was coming from. We did not keep a tab of time and before we knew it, we realized we were chatting for over six hours. One look at the watch alarmed us enough to rush out of the place.

He quickly dropped me home and I went straight to bed. I was tired and slept instantly. I decided to take his advice and have an honest conversation with Jeremy the next day and tell him how I really felt.

A BRAND NEW DAY THE SAME OLD STORY

I woke up the next morning only to find Rohan's message in my phone, "Good morning, sunshine". That brought an instant smile onto my lips. I loved how he always made me smile. It was the perfect start to the day. As I lay in bed looking at the message and smiling to myself, I realized today was the day I had to have the open and honest conversation with Jeremy. I was not really looking forward to it, but I knew it was something I needed to do.

I sent him a message saying I would call him and that I needed to talk. I was taken aback with his instant response as he usually took his own sweet time to respond. He said he would call me soon, himself. I began to feel a little positive about this whole conversation. Maybe he would actually understand.

I spent most of the morning waiting for his call, and just when I was preparing lunch, my phone rang. I answered in as cheerful a tone as possible, "Hello".

"Hi, Ali! So what is it that you wanted to talk to me about?"

"Well... Do you have time right now to like really talk, because it could take some time?" I asked, feeling nervous all of a sudden.

"Yes, tell me," he said, waiting for my response.

I had planned to call him but had not thought of what I was going to say. I was a little unsure and jittery at the thought of it. After a long pause, I finally spoke. "I wanted to talk about us."

"What about us?" He asked, sounding a little irritated.

The mildly harsh tone in his voice made me realize this was a bad idea after all, but I knew it was too late to turn back now and I had to take this conversation to an end, whatever it may be. So I mustered up the courage and spoke again.

"I want more," was all I could manage to say. The tone of my voice was oozing with nervousness.

He laughed, "What is more?"

"I don't want to share you," I said, realizing I had repeated Rohan's words.

"What's that supposed to mean? I don't get it." He asked, sounding puzzled.

"It means that I don't want you to be with other people."

"Hmmm…"

"I don't want to be with someone who doesn't want me to be his."

"I told you this would happen," he said, in a matter of fact tone which annoyed me no end.

"What the fuck is that supposed to mean?"

"I knew this conversation would come up, sooner or later."

"Well it has been almost two years, Jeremy. I think I'm justified in wanting more. I got into this thinking it was going somewhere." My words were dripping with frustration and my voice was growing louder with every sentence I said.

On the other side of the line, there was a brief pause. He didn't say anything.

"Jeremy, I don't understand it! You told me you love me, didn't you? Did I hear it wrong or does it mean something else to you?"

"I do love you but…"

"But what Jeremy? If you love someone, there is no but! Why did you bother becoming close to me and staying in touch and flying down to see me if you were never planning to commit. What was the point?"

I got so frustrated at his phlegmatic attitude that I didn't even wait for him to respond anymore and said blankly, "Let's just be friends".

Surprisingly, he responded immediately in a nonchalant tone, "If that's what you want, okay!"

I could not take it anymore. He was giving this 'If that's what I want' nonsense to me. I just told him what I fucking wanted and he didn't care.

I didn't really know what else to say at this point, so we said our goodbyes and ended the conversation.

This conversation had irritated me more than I could imagine. I didn't know what to think or say or do. All I knew was I didn't want to deal with it anymore. It was beyond me to understand how someone could be in love with someone, tell them that and yet can't be with them. For me, it's fucking black and white; you either want to be with someone or you don't. Telling someone you love them but can't be with them cannot be love. I was not sure why Jeremy had said those three words to me.

The conversation left me upset for most of my day and finally, when my anger died down, I messaged Rohan, saying, "I spoke to him. It didn't go well".

He replied soon after, "What happened? What did he say?"

"I don't really feel like typing all of it out. My anger will just come flooding back. Can I tell you when we meet?"

I was too irritated to talk about it and just wanted to get out of the house. Rohan always knew the right thing to say and everything seemed to be better with him around.

KISSES DON'T LIE

My irritation with the Jeremy episode was taking a toll on me. I threw my phone on the bed and stared at my watch in anger, wishing it to move faster so I could see Rohan. I was counting down the minutes to when I would see him because I desperately needed a friend.

And finally there was, one hour to go!

I had no idea how that hour would go by. I was ready to go, I was happy to just get out, yet agitated at the same time, and also didn't know what to do. I roamed about my room, wasted time online, and then watched television, and even messaged him telling him to meet me sooner. While all this was happening, or rather nothing was happening, Jeremy messaged me a "hey". After all that had happened in the morning, the only thing he says is "hey". Are you freaking kidding me!

I wanted to shout at him even in the SMS, but instead replied with a "hey" back; I didn't know what else to say to him.

He replied back instantly asking me how I was and what I was up to. I laughed because it amused me on how now that I said we should be friends, he remembered I existed and was putting in effort and taking some initiative.

I did not want to be mean or rude to him unnecessarily, so I politely responded, "okay. Not much, waiting for Rohan to pick me up".

His replies were quicker than I could ever imagine, but his remarks were still the same. He gave me his usual, "so you're spending a lot of time with him now, I see!"

Well I was, and I liked it. At least Rohan appreciated me and actually put in effort into making sure I knew it. I tried not to pick a fight and replied calmly, "he is a friend".

Just as I sent that, Rohan called to tell me that he was waiting outside.

I smiled to myself and jumped off the couch – handbag in one hand, phone in the other – and ran out the door.

I was genuinely happy to see him, and greeted him with a warm hug. Meeting him today was different. After what had happened with Jeremy, I was feeling free. Today, I was being myself. I was not trying to be 'just friends' or to pretend that I'm not was nervous around him. Nor was I going out of my way to tell him how I was beginning to feel for him. I was just being me.

This time when he asked what I wanted to do, the answer was simple – "Tequila".

He laughed when I said that and responded with an, "of course, whatever you want!"

I loved that about him; he always asked what I wanted to do. And not just for the heck of it, because he usually took it into consideration as well.

We headed to the same place where we had met for the second time. I had always loved the place and now it was extra special.

This time we danced and laughed and talked like there was no one else there, just the two of us. When they started to play, 'She will be loved' he moved close to me and we shared a slow dance. My body felt warm and comfortable against his. It felt like the right place to be, right here in his arms; my head pressed slightly against his chest while he held me gently.

"Want some more tequila?" He asked.

I was startled with the sudden question and a little embarrassed too. If only he knew what I was thinking.

"No, I'm good," I said.

The crowd was thinning out and people were leaving. I didn't want to go yet. I just wanted to stay there, where it seemed like everything would be all right and all my problems didn't exist.

Eventually we did have to leave. I was in no mood to go home though, so we decided to just talk for a while as we got into the car.

I lay my head against his shoulder, as I let out a loud sigh. He put his arm gently around me and asked, "So will you tell me now?"

"What am I supposed to tell you?" I was so lost in the moment I hardly remembered anything else.

"What happened with Jeremy?" He asked lowering his voice a little.

I stayed quiet for a while, just thinking where to begin telling him what had happened and what was bothering me. Finally, I told him everything.

"I called him to talk and tell him how I feel, and what I wanted. He just said the same thing he always does."

"Which is?"

"That he can't make any promises, which basically means that he might still meet other people."

"What do you mean?"

"Honestly, I have no idea what that is supposed to mean. I just don't get it. Am I not good enough for him?" I said, moving my head away from his shoulder and looking at him.

He didn't say anything, he just held my hand and looked right at me and said, "Don't ever say you're not good enough."

"I just wanted to be with someone who wants me back," I managed to say as I tried hard not to cry.

He sat there gazing at me. I got so lost in his eyes that without thinking, I said, "I wish I was with you."

I could not believe I had said that out loud. I was so embarrassed. I could feel my heart beat faster. I was nervous because I knew there was no way for me to take my words back. I was about to start panicking but I saw him smile and say, "That would be nice".

I smiled back, as I thought to myself how nice it would be.

"So what's happening with the two of you now?" He asked, bringing me back to reality.

"I don't know, I just didn't know what to say to him after a point of time and told him we should just be friends."

"That's not what you wanted." He said, as if checking to see if I had changed my mind.

"It seems like the best thing to do right now. I don't know what else to do."

"Why don't you try and work it out. You still want to."

"I can't deal with it right now." I sounded so confused to myself too.

"Hmm," he said thoughtfully.

Silence prevailed for a while as neither of us said anything. I lay my head on his shoulder, and stayed in the moment for a while. It seemed as if we both secretly liked each other, but neither of us said anything.

I moved away and sat back on my seat, realizing it was time to go home. My heart was still beating at superfast speed, the thuds being audible to my ears. I was beginning to have feelings for him.

As we entered the driveway to my house, my wish to spend some more time with him deepened. Just before I hopped off the car, he leant in to hug me and as we parted, the most amazing thing happened. We kissed. And my world stopped, along with everything else around me. And for that one moment, my heart felt like it was in the right place.

THE THINGS I FORGOT TO REMEMBER

I had begun to spend a lot of time with Rohan over the next few weeks. We ate dinner together and went for movies. The more time I spent with him the more I realized how similar we were and how we understood each other.

One morning, during breakfast, I stared at the bowl of cornflakes lying in front of me while I was dreaming about that kiss I had shared with him. Even though I was now friends with Jeremy and all that, I still felt a little guilty about it.

That didn't mean I was regretting the kiss in any way. It was so perfect. I felt like a teenager who had been kissed for the first time. Rohan had that effect on me. He reminded me of all those unrealistic childhood dreams I forgot to remember otherwise.

I suddenly jumped up from my chair, almost spilling my cornflakes, as I heard the loud banging of the kitchen door. I could see my younger sister Alisha walking right in, looking very disgruntled.

"What happened? What's with the door banging? You scared the hell out of me." I asked, wondering what her problem was.

"Oh, the usual! I was arguing with mom, *again*. She is driving me crazy and treating me like a child when I have no time for her lectures right now. You know I am not left with too much time; I'm in a rush and have so much to do before we leave. Anyway, you *do* remember we leave soon, right?" She asked, sounding just like our mother.

"Yes," I mumbled quietly. I had almost totally forgotten this trip to Mumbai with my sister. I had promised to help her shop. She was leaving for university soon and that too quite far off from India. Although she was annoying most of the time, but I also knew if I was ever doing something she thought was wrong or would hurt me later, she would not hesitate to say that to me in the most straightforward of ways. She looked out for me and after me in ways that made me forget which one of us was the older one. Although I'd never tell her that but I was sure to miss her.

When we had planned the Mumbai trip, I thought I would meet Jeremy and spend time with him. Now, since things were different, I was not sure about meeting him or even going to Mumbai at all for that matter.

I finished breakfast, picked up my phone and called Rohan as I walked into my room for some privacy.

He answered in a sleepy voice which sounded so sweet, "Hello."

"Did I wake you?"

"Yes but it is okay, I should be out of bed by now."

"Well then it's a good thing I called," I said.

"It's always a good thing when you call."

I smiled and began to blush a little. I was grateful that he could not see my cheeks turn red.

"So when do I see you next?" He asked, filling up the silence.

I could not wait to see him again.

"Soon... but umm... I might me going out of town for a few days. Till then, I'm all yours." My cheeks turned redder at the last line and I smiled a bit more.

"Where are you going?" His voice was suddenly more alert and the sleepiness vanished in a jiffy.

"My sister wanted to go to Mumbai to shop before she leaves for university and I had promised her I would go with her." After a brief pause I added, "And Jeremy is also there; so I had initially thought of meeting him too."

"Initially? So, now you won't meet him?" He asked, sounding like he hoped I would not.

"I don't know. I am still friends with him, so I might still meet him for a day. But to be honest, I'm still kind of confused about the whole thing."

"So you don't want to try and make it work anymore?"

"I don't know. It's just so complicated and I feel like I'm the only one trying to make it work, like he never really puts in much effort."

"You still really like him and you really wanted this. I think you should still try and make it work." Rohan's voice displayed total calmness and mine was just brimming with confusion and frustration.

"I do want to, but it's impossible to even have a proper conversation with him. He is so stubborn and closed to any other opinion other than his own."

"Why don't you try and fix it when you meet him. Maybe being with him and talking about it face to face will make it easier. You didn't really give him a chance when you talked to him. You told him you should be friends because you got irritated."

"I know and he said..." my voice trailed off.

"You never gave him the chance to tell you what he really wanted. Go there, talk to him, and give him that chance. He deserves at least that!"

"I don't know, let's see. I know I should. I'm not the type of person to just let things go so easily."

"Then why don't you try when you go there."

"It's so easy for him to let me go. He doesn't want to fight for me. It's like I'm the only one in it. He doesn't seem to care. Then why should I?"

He laughed a bit and said, "We have been friends for almost two months now and one thing I'm sure of is that you do care about him and maybe it will all seem different when you go there and speak to him in person. It could be because of the distance, for all you know. I think you should give it one more chance."

"Maybe I will." I paused to think over the entire situation and ended up saying, "You really are a good friend, Rohan. Thanks for being there."

"I should go now, Ali. Have to leave for work soon. Will we meet later tonight?"

"Yes, sure! But, can I ask you something before you go?"

"Sure," he said.

"Why are you being this nice to me and trying to help me with this whole Jeremy thing?" We both knew why I was asking him that question.

His voice was unexpectedly calm and composed as he said, "I know what you mean. It's just that despite everything, I think you're a good friend. I'm not used to having people as nice as you in my life, I like you and I want you to be happy. I'm just trying to do the right thing."

"Okay."

"So, will we meet later tonight?"

"Sounds good," I said, with a big smile on my face.

We said our goodbyes and hung up. But the smile remained for quite a while. He was a really nice guy. I knew he really liked me, yet he was convincing me to fix things with Jeremy and to do the right thing. That's what I loved most about him.

He was a friend to me before anything else.

GIVE ME A SIGN...SOME KIND OF DIRECTION

The realization that Rohan was right in suggesting that I should give it a shot was recurrent. I didn't want to be labeled a hypocrite; complaining about Jeremy not fighting to be with me on the one hand, and on the other, doing exactly the same myself.

I also knew that the tumultuous feelings I was developing for Rohan were not helping the situation. I guess I just needed time. I needed time enough to see if Jeremy would make efforts to be with me. All I needed was some kind of sign.

As that thought raced across my mind, my phone beeped showing Jeremy's message: "Hi, what's up?"

I laughed when I saw that. So it's true what they say about people: when you give someone space they wonder why you have lost interest in them all of a sudden and crave your attention more. Unthinkingly, my mind wandered to all the good morning messages I had sent him and had never got a reply. This was the first time he had taken an initiative to talk.

I replied saying, "Nothing much, was just about to go in for a shower".

A few seconds later he responded saying, "So am I disturbing you?"

I typed out "No, I'll go in while" and sent it.

His responses were quick, which was very unlike the Jeremy I knew. We continued to message each other for some more time. For the first time, it felt like he was making an effort to share his time with me; or even in his own quiet way, trying to tell me not to give up hope. I never doubted his words when he said he loved me; I knew he meant what he said. I just didn't understand why he was so afraid to show his love, or what was going through his head.

Although the messages were a good sign but I was still not sure. Maybe I could go there and see how things between us really were. Maybe it work out or maybe I was building it all up in my head. For over a month and half after the *friends* incident we hadn't spoken much and I wasn't sure if things would ever be the same again.

Only time would tell. The question was, how much time?

I reminded him in the next message that I was going to be in Mumbai in a few weeks. The moment that message status changed from 'pending' to 'delivered', my phone rang.

"Hello," I answered half laughing, because this change in his behavior and his sudden interest in me amused me a lot.

"Hello."

"So, I will be there soon" I said.

"I was planning to go on a holiday the day you arrive."

"Oh," I said, feeling a bit disappointed.

"I could postpone it by a day or so."

I was surprised when he said that. He was not one to change his plans. Maybe he really did miss me and was trying to make it work.

"You really mean that?" I asked, still a little surprised with this new Jeremy.

"Do I joke about these things?" He said in his usual Jeremy tone. This Jeremy tone of his was a mixture of sarcasm and matter-of-fact. It made me wonder at times if he was joking or serious. He always spoke in riddles which I never much cared for. Rohan on the other hand was always direct and honest; it was a refreshing change from always having to wondering and assume things never really knowing if you're wrong or right.

"You never know with you," I responded in a fed up tone. I was just tired with all the indirect communication.

He laughed, "And I thought you knew me."

"I thought so too," I said dryly.

"So, I *still* surprise you sometimes!"

I smiled; Jeremy would always be Jeremy. I liked that about him; the small unexpected things he did from time to time to bring a smile onto my face.

This suddenly reminded me of Valentine's Day earlier this year and how he had surprised me by buying me the perfect bracelet.. He knew that when it came to presents, I loved things I could always keep. The bracelet was something that would always keep him close to me, no matter where I was. He would do these little unexpected, meaningful things to make me happy, without my asking for it, and at times when I least expect them. It was this that made me forget my anger and frustration and made me feel I should give it one more chance.

Today, although I was not sure about making it work, yet, a part of me did not want to give up either. All said and done, Jeremy was a very honest and truthful guy and he was sincerely trying to change for me, for us. I liked this sudden change in his behavior; it was nice and positive.

"Yes, you still manage to surprise me," I said, smiling to myself.

"Glad to know I still have that effect on you, Ali."

I laughed at that totally Jeremy thing to say. "Effect it seems," I responded, as I rolled my eyes at the remark.

There was a brief pause and I knew he was smiling. After a moment he asked, "Where will you be staying?"

"My sister has made the bookings…"

He laughed, "Sounds fine, I will call you tomorrow and tell you my exact plans."

"Okay." I was happy with a conversation with Jeremy after a long time.

"Cool, I will see what I can do about my tickets and then I'll tell you."

"Sure, bye and thanks."

"What you thanking me for?"

"Changing your travel dates and tickets for me; I never thought you would."

"Hmm, like I said, I'm full of surprises."

I smiled, "Bye Jeremy."

"Bye."

I placed my phone carefully on the table and put it to charge before I went in for a shower.

FRIENDS AND KISSES

I spent the rest of the morning and most of the day with my sister. Time flies when two women sit together to make shopping plans. She asked me about Jeremy. I told her what was happening between Jeremy and me and that I would spend a day with him to fix things up. I knowingly left out the part about Rohan. I was not quite sure what to say to her about that yet, since I didn't know myself what was happening. And she would fire a million questions at me if I told her.

At around sundown, Rohan called to make plans. After spending ten minutes trying to figure out what we should do, we finally planned to catch up with our friends and go out drinking.

I spent a little over an hour to get ready, just in time for him to pick me up. I was happy every time I met him. No matter what my mood was before that, it always changed to happy.

As usual, minutes after reaching the lounge, Rohan had already ordered drinks for us. He walked up to me with four tequila shots in his hand and a huge grin on his face.

I laughed, "Stocking up?"

"No, just trying to make you smile."

I laughed as he gave me this look of accomplishment. After we finished the shots, I began to feel a little drowsy and I leant on him. He put his arms around me and made comfortable.

Being in this moment, relaxed and comforted, I began thinking how everything in my life was so confusing right now. At one end, I wanted to make things work with Jeremy. At the other end of things, every time I looked at Rohan, or I was with him it felt like I belonged with him. Sometimes I didn't know why I was trying to suppress the feelings I was beginning to have for him. To add to all this, now Jeremy was trying to make an effort to be with me, and be really good to me too, which made everything all the more confusing. I didn't know what to do anymore. There I was sitting next to a guy who perhaps once only existed in my dreams.

He looked right at me like he knew what I was thinking. This time I didn't avoid his gaze, and the next thing I knew, I was lost in his kiss again. It was like his lips told me secrets only I understood. This time I didn't move away. I didn't want to. I just wanted to hold on to the moment.

Just then my phone beeped loudly. It was a message from Jeremy saying he had re-booked his tickets.

I knew I should have felt guilty at this moment, but I didn't. I was not guilty at all. How could something so right and so perfect make me wish it didn't happen, even if for a second?

I knew this is not the way it should be.

Rohan saw me looking a bit distraught and asked what happened.

"I love kissing you, but what happened to being friends?"

"I don't know."

I smiled, "Neither do I."

"What's on your mind?" He asked, as we walked towards our table.

"It's just that Jeremy has started making an effort and I am a little confused. I don't know what to do."

Silence ruled for a while as we both sat on the couch there.

A while later he said, "Isn't that what you wanted? I thought you had decided you would go there and try and make things work."

The truth was I didn't know what I wanted anymore. I had been spending so much time with Rohan over the last two months and was beginning to develop feelings for him. Partly I felt it was the right thing to do, giving it a second chance with Jeremy. But my heart was beginning to lose interest. Sometimes it felt like a lost cause. Like I was fighting something that was just meant to be, I didn't know how to respond to his question.

"I don't know if this is going to make sense to you. The thing is I know what I'm going to do. Like go there and try and make it work. I told you earlier how I wanted a sign, and Jeremy making an effort just might just be that sign but I don't really know what I want."

"I'm not into the whole commitment, boyfriend thing either, I'm a little commitment phobic too but if you think there is something between you and Jeremy that you cherish, then don't give up on it. I just want you to be happy, and you should do whatever you do with confidence."

I didn't respond to that; what could I have said. We just changed the topic and continued to talk about other general things.

As we talked, I realized how much I really did like Rohan and loved that I could talk to him about anything. We kept talking, and more we talked, the more lost I was in his eyes. We stayed there until all I could think of was him. When I felt I won't be able to leave at all if I stayed any longer, we left. I knew I needed to control how I felt for him. Because it seemed like things might just work out with Jeremy; also because I didn't want to regret not giving it one last shot. I wanted to be sure.

The drive back home was quiet. Both of us could feel the tension but neither of us could do anything about it. The weather was romantic, the guy was perfect, and I could not do anything but pretend I wanted to be 'just friends'.

As he stopped the car right outside my house, neither of us wanting to leave, I lost myself in his kiss again.

"What happened to us being friends?" I asked again.

He moved back, looked straight ahead for a moment and then turned to me and said, "I have no idea. I can't seem to stay away from you."

I smiled because I felt the same way. This is perfect; this is what I wanted. This is how things should be. I knew I had Jeremy and I was going to go there and work things out, but what if?

Was this thing with Rohan mere attraction, or something more? Could this thing with Rohan possibly turn into love?

Although I was very comfortable with him, I needed to be sure. What if I leave everything I have with Jeremy for him and in the end it all comes down to nothing.

I was hoping this trip to Mumbai would help me figure it out.

CHOICES

It was finally time for me to leave for Mumbai. I was leaving the next day. I was not as excited as I thought I would be or should have been. I was too busy thinking about how I could spend as much time with Rohan as possible before I left. I didn't want to leave just yet. I wanted to waste away my time with Rohan because I was afraid once I left, that would be the end of it for Rohan and me.

The next morning, I was restless because I wanted to see him before I left. I made plans with Rohan and our friends for the evening. That's when my sister barged into my room to yell at me for not having started to pack.

"You have not packed yet? You've not even begun!" She yelled, sounding like a high-pitched chimpanzee.

"I will. There's still a day" I said with an attempt to sound reassuring, which clearly didn't work.

"This coming from you, who usually packs one week in advance?" She responded in a suspicious tone.

I smiled slightly, as I thought of Rohan for that moment. He was the reason I wanted to stay and not go anywhere.

"Okay, what is it? Spill the beans. I know there is something you're not telling me." She sounded upset.

"Well, okay. It's nothing much. I met this guy some months ago and it's actually a little soon to say anything, but I do like really like him. I'm not sure what it is but I just can't get him out of my mind. And things with Jeremy have not been going too well lately. So I don't know exactly what to do. Now Jeremy has started making an effort to make things better, and here I like this other guy. I don't even know if he is worth risking everything I have with Jeremy yet. So I have been thinking that maybe this trip will help me figure out what to do and make a decision."

She made a strange face and said, "This explains why you have not packed and why you have been in a better mood these days. I mean you have been extra nice to me too. You always smile randomly and you have been going out more than you usually do.

"What are you plans with Jeremy then?"

"Like I said, when I go there I will figure it out."

"I think you should decide once and for all about Jeremy. I think it's been too long now," she sounded annoyed.

"But what if..."

"Enough of your what ifs. He has been with you almost two years and he isn't ready to commit. Just figure it out. Make most of this trip and spend some time by yourself. That'll help you know what you really want. Also, Aleah, everyone deserves to be with someone who wants to be with them, and not someone who is almost always unsure."

She walked out of the room with a smile, but her words stayed in my head and taunted me all day.

I went into my room thinking I would start packing; instead I lay there on my bed staring at the ceiling wondering what to do. All thoughts escaped me but one; Rohan.

I was startled with my phone ringing really loudly right next to my ear. The annoyance of the volume vanished when I saw Rohan's name flashing on the screen.

"Hi! I will be there in twenty minutes."

Twenty minutes! I looked to check what the time was. I had been sleeping for four hours!

"Okay, will be ready."

"Why do you sound so lost? Are you okay?"

"Oh yes! I just dozed off. But now, I'm up!"

"Wake up, you have to see me."

The size of my smile, tripled. "I know; can't wait."

He hung up but the smile it left on my face felt great. He was just so adorable. How could I not want to be with someone like that? I jumped out of bed and into the shower and was ready in record time, much to my surprise.

When I got into the car, the first thing he said was, "You're ready!"

I laughed, "Impressed?"

"A little, I thought I would have to wait."

"I was just so excited to see you" I said in a half mocking half serious tone, with a grin on my face.

He just leaned in and kissed me gently on my cheek. I blushed and wondered how he managed to make me smile this way, always?

But there was a heavier weight on my mind and I wanted to get rid of it first.

"Rohan, I need to talk to you about something." I said.

"Sure, what's on your mind?"

"I like you and I can't do this the way it is. I think I need to choose. What I'm saying is, I think I need to make a decision once and for all about us."

"Choose what?"

"Choose, between you and Jeremy."

"Hmmm, what exactly do you mean?"

"I mean, I need to go and either fix things with him or leave him."

"You should fix it. That's what you've always wanted."

He made it a point to mention that I was the one who wanted it every time the topic was raised. I liked it initially but now I just wished he'd say he wanted to be with me. I knew he wanted me, but I wished he would tell me to choose him. Like admit it out loud or something.

"Honestly, I'm not really sure if I know what I want anymore, but I do think I should give it a shot."

"Why are you not sure?"

"I like you," I said, trying to avoid eye contact. I was feeling nervous and vulnerable for that moment as I finally admitted how

I felt about him, out loud. Those words I knew I couldn't take back.

"I like you, too."

"A lot," he added, after a brief pause.

I smiled.

He always knew how to put me at ease. He liked me too; I was so happy. I was a teeny bit worried that it would be one of those things where he would not say anything and it would just get all awkward.

But it did not, and he said it back.

"Ali, go to Mumbai and figure out what we need to. Like you said, if things works out with Jermy then whatever this thing is that's started between us we will stop it and be friends. If things don't when your back we will take it from there. Just be happy."

CAN'T SEEM TO STAY AWAY

I don't know what it is about you.
I can't seem to stay away.
The way you look at me.
The way I look at you.
I get lost in the moment.
It's like no one else is there.
The smiles I hide, the words almost spoken.
The yearning to show you; how much you mean to me.
And yet, not show too much.
You're so close.
But I can't have you.
I try to distract myself; I look away.
I wish I could tell you, I think this is crazy.
I wish I could tell you, I wish this is real.
I wish I could kiss you.
I wish I could keep you.
I don't know what it is about you.
I can't seem to stay away.

LEAVING ON A JET PLANE

It was for the first time, and hopefully the last, that I had a few minutes left for my airport check-in, and I had only just finished packing. Soon enough, we were rushing out the door. Although I did want to finally fix things with Jeremy, I didn't like the thought of leaving Rohan behind. It felt like my heart was at two places at once, if such a thing is possible.

Just before boarding my flight, I called Rohan up. We spoke for a while and somehow it felt like goodbye. I felt the moment I would get on that plane, everything would change.

When we landed in Mumbai, the smell of the air was so familiar. There was a slight feeling of nostalgia. This was the city where Jeremy and I had met in the first place. It had been a long time since then and so much had changed.

Once we got into the cab we gave the driver clear instructions as to where we wanted to go.

Once we were on the way to the hotel, I put my headphones on and drowned into the sound of blaring music; I looked out the window and watched the traffic move at snail's pace.

I had not even finished listening to one song when my sister pulled out the headphones from my ears and started asking me about Jeremy.

"So, what's the status of things between you and Jeremy now?"

"I don't know. I'm planning to give it one more shot while I'm here."

"Are you sure it's worth it?"

Every time anyone asked me that, it made me think twice. I had lost the conviction I once had about my relationship with Jeremy.

"I think I owe it to the relationship." I guess I was just trying to do the right thing.

My sister looked at me with this 'don't you try and fool me' look and said, "Since when have you become so practical? I know you have been hurt before, but this is not the way it should be and you know that."

"I know, but there is nothing I can do."

"Yes there is; just leave. Don't be with someone who doesn't have the fucking balls to make you his girlfriend."

"He needed time to be sure."

"He had his time. If he doesn't know by now, he will never know."

I knew she was right, but I didn't want to just give up. If you love someone, you fight for them. That's what I believed. Besides what's the harm in giving it just one last shot. It's not like I knew for sure that things with Rohan would work. Besides he clearly said he was not into the whole commitment thing either. However I could not help how I felt and in time would know where my heart lies. Though honestly, I think I already knew the answer to that question; I just needed to be sure too.

I wanted to use this time with Jeremy to see how I felt about him. To see how much I still wanted to be with him.

"I want to make sure, because if I leave I won't go back."

"I guess that makes sense," she said.

"I want to make this decision taking Rohan out of the picture. I don't want to leave Jeremy because of the feelings I have for Rohan."

"But you do have feelings for Rohan. That's not going to change."

I didn't know how to respond to that. Neither of us said much for the rest of the drive.

After checking into the hotel and freshening up, my sister dropped me off to Jeremy's house on her way to her mall. We still didn't say much, until I reached Jeremy's house. The only thing my sister said to me as I got out of the car was "Just be happy".

I knew she meant well. I smiled and waved goodbye as I disappeared into the building.

ON THE OTHER SIDE OF THE DOOR

I was nervous as I pressed the doorbell and stood there outside Jeremy's door. He opened the door and greeted me with a hug. It felt nice and unexpected. But somehow his hugs didn't feel as warm as they used to, or maybe it was all in my head.

When I walked into his room, I noticed there were clothes everywhere, like a bachelor's apartment. It seemed as if a tornado had hit.

"What happened here?"

"I was packing and folding clothes, trying to make the house look nice for you," he explained.

I laughed, as a picked up some of the clothes and started to fold them.

He smiled and went into the other room.

After I was done folding whatever unfolded clothes I could lay my hands on, I went to help him pack. It was funny to watch him pack. His room was almost always so messed up and disorganised; yet, when it came to packing, he had lists with exactly what he wanted to take with him.

I helped him pack as much as I could but, then after a while, I don't know why but I started missing Rohan and could not get him off my mind. It made me a little uneasy. I couldn't help myself and decided to call him. Jeremy was busy packing.

I took my phone and went to the next room. I could not wait to hear his voice as I speed dialled his number. He picked up in a few rings and my heart skipped a beat when he said, "Hello".

"Hey," I responded, trying real hard to curb my enthusiasm.

"How come you called? I thought you would be busy with Jeremy?"

I was not sure if he was being sarcastic when he said that. "I am at his house, but I felt like talking to you, so I called," and that was the truth.

"How come? Don't you want to spend time with him?"

This time I knew it was not sarcasm. It was that curiosity he had, where he had to always know what I was thinking. "I don't know, maybe I was missing you, I guess."

"But, you are with him, how do you have time to miss me?"

I laughed, "Well, I still do."

I didn't know how to explain to him how crazy this was and how I myself didn't really know what was going on or how to feel. What I did know was that I missed him.

We continued to talk for a while, and then I realised it had almost been half an hour. I hung up and told him I would talk to him again soon and then went back in the room where Jeremy was almost done packing. He didn't ask me where I had been, but some part of me knew he already knew the answer to that question.

After he finished packing, we decided to go shopping and grab a bite to eat. We decided to eat at McDonalds which is where we had gone when we first had dinner together. Once we ordered our food and sat down, I noticed he was smiling.

"Why are you smiling?" I asked him.

"I was remembering the first time we came here."

I blushed; that was such an embarrassing moment.

"Don't blush; it's okay. I found it cute when you took really long to eat and tried hurrying up because I was done eating."

"Hmm...," I couldn't help but smile.

"That was the first time we had dinner together, right?"

"Yes, that was a very unromantic first date."

He laughed, "Well, I made up for that the last time, didn't I?"

"True! But the question is, will you keep it up?" I said along with 'that's more like an order' sort of look.

He laughed.

It began to feel like things were a little like they used to be and were slowly falling back into place. I decided that tomorrow before I left, I would ask him if he wanted to make this work. Maybe he'd say yes.

TWO PLACES AT ONCE

When we reached back, I was really hoping I would get to spend time with him. I needed to know if there was something to hold on to or if I was still imagining this amazing relationship that we could have and building it up in my head when in reality it was just another castle in the air. I had a tendency to do that, to consider only the best in people, only to be let down later.

Jeremy interrupted my thoughts as he passed me my phone saying, "Payal is calling you." I took the phone from him and spoke to her. Once I hung up, I turned to Jeremy. Before I could say anything he looked at me and said, "Your friends want to spend time with you then you should go".

"Yes, is that okay?" I asked a little worried that my excitement may have forced him into saying that and I knew we had planned to spend the evening together.

"Yes."

"Thank you."

Just before leaving I went to get ready and as I stood there under the shower, I thought finally some alone time. As the water trickled down my body I let my mind wonder off and yet again I found myself thinking about Rohan. I just could not get him out of my mind. I missed him. I missed his kisses. I missed the feeling I got when I was with him, like it could never get better than this. I missed the way I always lost track of time when I was with him, and how goodbye was always seemed so difficult even when I knew I would see him again really soon. Sometimes I thought that if I was going to see him again soon then I should not have to leave him at all I could just stay.

I got startled when I heard Jeremy bang loudly on the bathroom door. I had this slight sinking feeling and I felt bad that I was here with Jeremy and I could not stop thinking about Rohan but I didn't know how to stop. I quickly finished my shower and then left.

I had missed Mumbai and my friends here. It was nice spending time with them.

After dinner with my friends as I walked back towards the apartment, I began to think about me and Jeremy, about the fate of our relationship. The truth is that I had been with him for long enough and had planned so much for the future with him in mind that I didn't know if it was *that* which was making give it one last chance despite his unwillingness to commit. I had an almost perfect guy that I could not get my mind off. A guy who wanted to be with me and was not afraid to show it; a guy who told me he would never want to share me. Someone who made my heart skip a beat without any effort. Someone who made my world come to a standstill when he was around me and someone who's company I enjoyed so much I lost all sense of time. I was not sure anymore what was stopping me from taking a chance with Rohan. I was just so afraid about the way he made me feel. I had previously only heard about such feelings in books or movies. It was too amazing a feeling to be true.

Once I was back at the apartment it was just the two of us. I was wondering if I should talk to him today or leave it for the next day. I wanted to talk to him and decide once and for all if there was a future with him worth holding on to.

We both sat on the couch and he switched the television on as if by habit. We left it on a music channel and just sat there neither of us said anything as song after song kept playing. After a while, he moved closer and I leaned back into his arms.

I closed my eyes for a moment as I lay back into his arms. The moment I shut my eyes, I had a vivid image of when I was sitting in the car with Rohan. Somehow when I was with him I felt so safe, like nothing could ever harm me. I don't know why all these thoughts and images were coming to me now, at perhaps one of the most inappropriate times, but I couldn't help it. I tried not to smile as I thought about Rohan, and how every time I sent him some song that reminded me of him, he would always play it when we were together. I couldn't control it any longer. I could not hold back and a smile finally did escape my lips.

Jeremy gave me this quizzical look as he asked, "What was that smile for?"

I blushed because I could not tell him what I was thinking. I looked away, towards the television and said, "Just like that! It's nice to be here, that's all."

You know that feeling when you're lying and you choke on your words; I did. And felt a little guilty.

A few minutes later, I thought it was time one of us said something and broke the deafening silence. The moment I was about to speak, Jeremy leant in to kiss me.

A horde of emotions flooded my heart as the thought of Jeremy kissing me sank in. It felt like I was cheating on Rohan; but how could that be? How can one cheat on someone they are not even with? Yet I had this really horrible feeling. I tried to ignore it and be present in that moment with Jeremy. But I could not get Rohan out of my head. Was I going mad or did I just not have my heart with me anymore?

When you're with someone and you can't stop thinking about someone else, you know there is no going back from there. This had to stop and I needed to clear things with Jeremy once and for all. My heart could not be at two places at once. I needed to let Jeremy go. Although I had made up my mind to do it, yet I was scared because I knew there'd be no turning back.

LIKE IT'S THE LAST TIME

The next morning, my sister woke me up.

"How come you came back so early last night?"

"I couldn't have the conversation. I'm going there for breakfast now will talk to him then."

"Good luck."

I smiled. I really did need the luck.

I picked up breakfast for the two of us on the way to Jeremy's house. While I sat at the table eating breakfast, he was frantically walking up and down the house completing his last minute packing as he had his flight in a few hours. I tried to get him to have breakfast with me and called out to him several times, but he was too busy packing to even look up from his suitcase.

When I was done with breakfast, I finally chased him around the house trying to get him to eat something by shoving food down his throat any moment I got. He pinned me down with an intense stare, with an extremely naughty look on his face and sparkling glint in his eyes.

"What's with that look?" I asked him.

"Are you always this nice or …?" His voice trailed off into silence and his lips curved into a half smile.

"I'm usually like this with people I care about, you know," I said as I gave him 'you should already know that' look.

He laughed, "Thank you. Most people don't do all this."

"What can I do if you have just been with all the wrong people?"

He smiled. "You always have to say something, don't you? Can't you simply accept a compliment like a normal person?"

I laughed, "Not used to it, you know."

He leant in and slowly whispered, "I love you".

I smiled and felt guilty at not having said it back.

It was almost time to leave and say our goodbyes for now. I still had not brought up the conversation. The fact that he said he loved me made me wonder again. Just as Jeremy had to leave, my sister called.

"Hi, where are you?" I asked.

"Downstairs waiting for you, are you ready?" She asked sounding very impatient.

"Yes, see you in a minute."

I walked up to Jeremy to say bye and hugged him. He held me for a while, longer than he usually did. It was like he knew this was the last time he would get to hold me in his arms.

CLARITY

Once I got into the car, I thought of texting Jeremy saying, "nice meeting you this time". I thought this could be like a starting over thing.

Before I could even press the send button, my sister piped in, "How was it?"

I laughed and asked her to wait for a second. Gosh! she was always in such a hurry to know everything. I sent the message and turned toward her, still laughing at the curious look on her face. I finally told her what she'd been waiting to hear, "It was good! I think maybe it's time to let Jeremy go."

She gave me a very suspicious look and muttered, "Are you sure this is what you want?"

That question had scared me so much till this moment. But this time it didn't. I had decided this and believed this was good for me. "Yes. It didn't feel the same. This time when he leant in to kiss me I moved away and even when he told me he loved me I couldn't say it back. Over these last couple of months things seemed to have just changed. It's for the best," I said.

Just as I said that, my phoned beeped. I thought Jeremy would have replied, but it was not. It was Rohan and my heart skipped a beat, again. I could not stop smiling.

"Jeremy?" my sister asked raising an eyebrow.

"Rohan," I replied.

She grabbed my phone from my hand and read some of the messages Rohan had sent me earlier. She gave me a 'you're such an idiot' look as she returned my phone.

"What was that look for?" I asked.

"He misses you," she replied with a smirk.

I blushed and I could feel my cheeks turn red. I read his message and smiled to myself as I replied with "I miss you too; more than you realize".

I did miss him and a lot more than I should have. I knew that I had half decided to stay with him, to choose him. I was just not ready to tell him that yet. I could not wait to go back and see him again. I was also a little annoyed that Jeremy had not replied to my message yet.

"Lost in thought?" my sister asked.

"Just wondering…" I said.

"About what?" she asked with a slightly worried look in her eyes, possibly fearing I was confused about Jeremy again.

"I don't know I have this extremely uneasy feeling. Like what if I have made the wrong decision?" I asked. Saying that out loud made me feel even more uneasy.

"I think you have made the right decision. I have been trying to tell you for so long if he is not willing to commit after almost two years it's not worth it. Have you told either of them yet what you have decided?" She made everything seem so simple with her words when honestly, nothing about this decision was simple; this decision would change my life and all that I had planned for the future would be lost. It was about the rest of my life versus taking a chance. Any decision I'd take would change everything for me. How was I supposed to know Rohan would not end up being just another guy?

I decided to stop thinking about it. I was just getting more and more confused. Maybe my sister was right; maybe this was the best decision I had made in a while and it was the right thing to do.

People say 'you should follow your heart and your heart knows no disappointment'; at this moment, I really hoped that was true.

A loud beep diverted my mind from my thoughts. Rohan had replied saying, "That's a good thing. You should miss me". I smiled.

Maybe it really was a good thing. I replied back saying, "Of course it is. I just didn't think I would miss you this much".

Just as it got delivered, he had already sent, "Come back soon".

"I will. Can't wait to see you again, I miss you." Part of me wished I could take the next flight out but I knew my sister would kill me if I even thought about it. So I knew I had to wait, till I could see him again. Plus I needed a day to just absorb the decision I had almost made.

"Then come back soon," he replied, this time with a cute sad smiley face at the end.

I smiled at that and typed, "I will, as soon as I can."

"When is that?" He asked.

"Day after," I replied.

As soon as I hit the send button, my sister started speaking to me in a motherly tone, "I really don't know why you're confused or doubtful. It's pretty simple the way I see it. I mean seriously, you're telling me you're not sure if you should be with Rohan? Look at your smile; you could easily beat any love-sick teenager."

"It's not that I'm not sure. If Jeremy was not in my life, I would have been with Rohan in a heartbeat. Just a little scared to take a chance." I hoped she'd understand what I meant.

"You know you want to be with him, I don't understand why you're afraid. The way Rohan is with you from all these messages I have seen, he really likes you. You're not going to find a guy like this easily. It's not every day you find someone who makes your heart skip a beat or gives you butterflies almost every single time you talk. People spend their whole lives looking for a love of this sort. You have it right in front of you. You should grab hold of him and never let go. I know I'm making it sound dramatic but you get my point."

"Well, this is reality you know. I know it feels like a fantastic fairy tale but this is real life."

"I know and you're lucky to have someone like this in your 'real life'," she said in a sarcastic tone.

I laughed.

She continued, "I'm not saying it's going to be perfect. No relationship is. I agree there is nothing called magic. But you can make your own fairy tale come true if you give it a chance."

We were quite for some time: she looked out of the window thinking I don't know what, and me looking at her knowing she was going to say something more.

Finally my sister spoke again, "Think about it, you have been trying to make it work with Jeremy. It's been fifteen minutes and he still hasn't replied to your message. On the other hand, Rohan has not only messaged several times but has got you smiling like an idiot. I guarantee you have made the right decision."

"I know," I responded so quietly. I was not even sure she heard it.

A few seconds later, I was smiling again as I read Rohan's message saying, "That's too far," this time followed by two sad smiley faces.

My sister was right; he had got me smiling like an idiot.

"I know baby, but I will see you the day I get back. Okay?" I replied knowing exactly how he felt. It did seem far away.

"Okay. I know this is a month's notice but you have to spend New Year's Eve with me," he wrote. I could feel his eagerness as I read the message.

I didn't know what to say to that; spending New Year's Eve with him would be a big deal for me. While I was wondering what to type back, the doorman of our hotel opened the car door for me. I was so wrapped up in him I didn't even realize we had reached. As I got out of the car, I texted saying, "I've reached the hotel. I will call you soon."

All said and done, I was sure of one thing. It definitely *was* time for me to take my friendship with Rohan to the next level.

GOODNIGHT BABY

It had been about four hours since I texted him; it was nearly dinner time and Jeremy still had not replied. This only convinced me more that I had made the right decision. It was only much later, when I was half way through dinner, when Jeremy replied.

I didn't know if I was more disappointed that he took so long to reply or that his message was as good as not sending anything at all. He sent another "what's up?" I didn't know if I should laugh or go hunt him down and slap him. I was so totally pissed off.

I was now completely and one thousand percent sure of my decision.

As I got up and walked towards the bed, my sister sensed there was something on my mind and asked me about it.

"Oh, nothing! Jeremy replied with what's up and it annoyed me. I guess after you spend a day with someone who you usually don't get to see, you expect a little more than *that*!"

This time, even she didn't have anything to say. She would always go on and on about how she was right, but this time her silence spoke louder than words.

"The good news is I'm sure of decision now." I said.

She looked at me, rolling her eyes, "you're crazy".

I simply stuck my tongue out at her and started looking for something to watch on TV.

"What are we watching?" She asked.

"I don't know," I said, as I kept flipping through the channels, not able to find anything to watch. I decided to crash into bed for the day and turned the television off, put the remote on the bedside table and buried my head deep into my pillow.

"You're going to sleep?" My sister asked.

"Yes, hope for a better day tomorrow. Goodnight."

"Goodnight, sleep well and stop thinking about Jeremy. He is not worth it. See you in the morning, I'm off to my room," she said, as she walked towards the door and shut it behind her with a loud thud.

It had been almost an hour-and-a-half and I still could not sleep. I had been tossing and turning in bed. Something felt incomplete. About another half an hour later, I was still sleepless. I picked up my phone to check the time and found myself calling Rohan.

"Hello," he answered on the first ring, as if he was expecting my call.

"Hey, are you busy or can you talk?" I asked, mostly because I was nervous and had no idea what to say.

"No, I always have time for you," he said.

The moment I heard that, a smile escaped from my lips automatically. Making me smile always came easy to him. "You should," I replied.

"I should? Really… telling me what I should do now."

"Yes. Am I not allowed to? It's called the three month privilege."

He laughed, "You are. What're you doing?"

"Nothing much. In bed; was going to sleep, thought I'd call you."

"How are things with Jeremy? How did it go?" he asked in a little more serious tone.

"It was okay."

"So that means once you're back, we go to being 'just friends'?" He asked sounding a little less happy now.

Before I could even respond to that, Rohan continued with a gentle, "It's okay. I understand. It's good; this is what you wanted and you should be happy. I want you to be happy."

I couldn't help but laugh. I didn't really know what to say or how to explain to him what was really going on and how I felt, so I just said, "Thank you" followed by, "I'm here now. Not back yet." I myself didn't know what I was trying to say. I was just not ready to share my decision yet. I wanted to first tell Jeremy it was completely over.

"So you're saying you're mine for the next two days?" he asked sounding all hopeful.

I laughed but the sadness in my voice was easy to spot when I said, "I miss you".

"I miss you too," he said with exactly the same hint of sadness in his voice.

It was like we both felt exactly the same way but neither of us knew what to do about it. "I should go to bed now," I said not really wanting to.

"I wish I could join you," he said in his usual cute, excited tone.

I laughed.

"Come back soon, okay baby," he said.

"I will, soon," I said and added a quick "Goodnight".

"Goodnight baby."

I loved it when he called me baby. I loved being his baby. I wish I could continue being his baby. Jeremy never really called me anything sweet at all.

"Dream about me," I said smiling.

"I always do," he said in a sweet low voice before disconnecting.

I put my phone back near my pillow and finally was able to sleep. There was something comforting about Rohan, almost always. I used to feel the same about Jeremy too at times, but he always had this stand-offish thing about him; when I was not physically present with him, I was just another girl to him.

Rohan, on the other hand, no matter how far or close, made sure I never left his thoughts or his heart.

MY HEART IS YOURS TO LOVE OR BREAK

The next day, I woke up at lunch time and the first thing I did was message Rohan "Good morning". I was getting out of bed when my sister walked into my room looking annoyed that I had not finished with lunch and wasn't even ready for that matter. I had promised to spend the last day of the trip with her, shopping. We were supposed to be out by eleven and I had just woken up. I was so absorbed in my own thoughts that I was practically unaware of anything around. Just when I thought she was done yelling, she picked up my phone, looked at it, and started off again.

"You always have time to message Rohan."

"It's just one message," I said rolling my eyes. "Let me go have a shower and then we will leave okay?" I calm her down.

"What about lunch?" She asked, attempting to be concerned but really more worried that we would not have enough time to shop.

"We will pick up something on the way," I said knowing that would calm her down a little; it worked and she cheered up. Sisters!

As I gathered my things and walked into the bathroom for a shower, I asked my sister to pick out something from my suitcase for me to wear because I knew if it was up to me, I would spend at least half-an-hour doing so.

She yelled from outside to tell me that she had picked out clothes for me added with a naughty tinge in her voice, "And by the way, your lover boy messaged saying good morning with a kiss, and he also said it was nice talking to you last night." Her voice lowered as she completed the sentence.

Then all of a sudden there was a loud banging on the bathroom door which made me pick up my foot cream instead of my toothpaste. "What's wrong with you, crazy woman?" I yelled.

"You spoke to Rohan last night?"

"Yes."

"What's going on?" She asked, forgetting all about the shopping plan.

"Nothing," I responded, trying to sound casual and usual.

"Don't give me that. You wake up and the first thing you do is message Rohan and you're saying 'nothing'. What was your response to the message Jeremy sent you last evening by the way?"

"I didn't reply. I forgot." I said feeling slightly embarrassed.

"I told you. You only remember Rohan; nothing else."

"Very funny," I said as I barged out of the bathroom almost knocking her over in irritation.

"What are you so irritated about?" She asked as if I was not allowed be annoyed.

She added a snide remark saying, "I was right."

She always knew what exactly she needed to say to strike that nerve. I sat on the edge of the bed still wrapped in my towel, my hair dripping wet. I could feel the drops of water roll down my back.

"What exactly happened with Jeremy when you were with him?" She asked.

I wasn't really expecting her to ask me that. It was out of the blue but I answered anyway. "It was actually not that bad and he was nice to me."

"But…" my sister added.

"But, I told you I didn't feel the same and when I was with him, I kept thinking about Rohan." I felt really embarrassed when I said that.

She sat next to me and hugged me a moment and then said, "If you want my opinion, which is free for you, here's what I think."

After a pause she added, "I think that you have feelings for Rohan and not just regular feelings. I think you really like him and you feel strongly about him. I'm not saying you're in love with him. I'm just saying there is something there and it's different the way you are with him. I have known you since you were born and the last time you felt like this was the first time you fell in love. You were with that guy for what, four years and since then this is the first time you have been this happy when it comes to relationships that is. I have seen someone have this effect on you after so freaking long.

"Truth is, you have feelings for Rohan, the really strong I want to fall in love with you type feelings. But you're trying to control it more than you need to. Stop doing that, stop pretending, only then will you be happy."

Truth is a matter of perception; we only see what we are prepared to confront. I thought about what she said for a while, "But that's the thing. That's what I'm afraid of, it always starts out nice and three or four months down the line everything changes. He won't want me anymore or get bored. I fear the possibility of my heart breaking again."

"Ali, nothing has ever been certain with Jeremy. He takes you for granted. I'm not saying he is not a nice guy. I understand that he is very marriage-able and you guys are right for each other in a lot of ways but love is not one of them. I know that somewhere deep in your heart you wanted to get out of this relationship too. You have just been afraid to. Maybe Rohan coming into your life is god's way to remind you that you deserve someone who feels the same way about you and you do about them."

She was right. "What if I do give Rohan a chance and it doesn't work out and then I realize I made a mistake. He told me he was commitment phobic."

She looked at me with a really serious expression. "If you stay with Jeremy, especially right now, that would be a mistake too. Forget Jeremy and forget Rohan for a moment and tell me what *you* want?"

"I want someone who wants me back. Someone who will fight for me and who loves me and will always show me how much." I saw a smile creep on my sister's face when I said that.

"I don't know much about your relationships but from what I see, Rohan wants to be with you and he isn't afraid to show you how he feels. I think you would be happy with him and you should give it a shot. Where is the hopelessly romantic girl I once knew?"

I laughed, "I know what you mean. With Rohan it does feel like it's the first time I'm falling in love or giving someone my heart without any questions because it feels natural. Like it's meant to be or something. I can't believe I'm saying this," I said with a blush creeping up to my cheeks.

"I think you have already given him your heart. You just need to do something about it now."

I smiled, feeling a mix of anxiety and relief and asked her, "So, what do I do now?"

"Do what you feel like. You have made your choice; you just need to follow through."

"Okay," I said as I laughed, my sister was behaving like a grandmother.

"Good," she replied decisively.

"Let's go shopping now. I will deal with this before I go to bed. I need to just absorb or accept – or whatever the word is – first."

She smiled, and picked up my dark blue denim shorts and chucked them at me, asking me to hurry up.

I got up to get ready. I felt so much better. This was perhaps one of the most important decisions I had to make. I knew this decision was about to change my life. Letting someone into my heart and allowing them to get to know the *real* you was something I rarely ever did.

THE CHANCES WE ARE MEANT TO TAKE

After hours of shopping were over, I was so exhausted I didn't even feel my feet. I loved shopping; it always relaxed me and took my mind off most of the mundane happenings and complications of everyday life.

The moment I entered the hotel room, I dropped my shopping bags in one corner of the room and collapsed into the soft and extremely sinkable mattress. It was time now. I knew I had to deal with my complicated love life and un-complicate it.

I decided to call Jeremy first. As usual, I called him up twice but there was no answer from his end. I just wanted to get over with this so I messaged him saying, "I think we should just be friends, we are better off like that". The bastard actually replied saying "sure". It was that fucking easy for him to let me go. He didn't even think twice. I was glad I had decided to leave him. It was finally over. I was relieved.

I was also excited that I could now be with Rohan without anything holding me back. I couldn't wait to call Rohan and tell him.

I had another quick shower, got into comfortable clothes and crashed into bed. I was all ready and pretty excited to call him. As I dialled his number, I could feel my heart beat as loud as a drum.

"Hey" he answered.

"Are you busy?" I asked, sounding a little too excited. I think he could hear the excitement in my voice.

"A little, but tell me what happened?"

"I told Jeremy that we'll just be friends and that it'll be better that way," I said a little anxious about his response.

"Really? And what did he say?"

"All he said was okay; like it really doesn't matter to him. He didn't even fucking bother to fight for me."

"How come, though?"

"How do I know why he won't fight for me; obviously he doesn't care. I was stupid to think he did, and for the long time that I did."

"I meant, why did you decide to be friends?"

"Oh", I said feeling a little embarrassed. "I don't know, I guess he was not making the effort and my heart was not really in it."

"Your heart was not in it? I thought you wanted to get married to him?"

"I did but...he doesn't want to commit and..." after a brief pause I added, "I met you and said you said you won't share me. That kind of stuck with me." I couldn't help blushing.

"I would never share you."

"I know that's why I like you so much."

"I really like you too baby."

"You should," I said, with a big smile on my face. Everything was now the way it should be.

"When are you back? When do I see you?"

"Tomorrow," I said all excited.

"Will you spend New Year's Eve with me?"

My happiness doubled, rather tripled, when he asked me that. "It's a month away!"

"Just answer the question."

"Of course, I would love to." I was even more excited to go back. I could not wait to see him.

"Call me when you land tomorrow. Okay? "

"Okay. I can't wait."

"Me too."

"Bye baby."

"Bye."

"I miss you."

I loved it when he said that. Jeremy had never said any such sweet things to me. "I miss you too. See you soon."

"It's still far away," he said in a voice that sounded like a four-year-old boy's. He sounded cute when he spoke like that.

"It's not that far. It's less than 24 hours."

"I know but still it feels far."

I laughed, "I know, tomorrow."

"Okay, Bye."

"Bye."

This was going to be the best New Year's Eve ever. There was no way more perfect to spend time with him and begin whatever this was. Just one month to go.

ALL YOU NEED IS LOVE

I woke up the next morning, completely eager and excited to get back home and meet Rohan. You know that feeling when you wonder what you were doing all your life and why you didn't meet him earlier.

Before I even brushed my teeth or showered, I messaged Rohan and said, "Good morning. I'm so excited to get back and meet you. I missed you so much, you have no idea. I don't even know if it's possible to miss anyone this much, at least I never have before, can't wait to see you".

I was so happy. I don't think I had ever packed all my things so fast before. I was ready in no time with half an hour to spare before I had to leave for the airport. I looked at my phone hoping Rohan had replied but he had not. Rohan was probably asleep.

I didn't know what to do with my half hour. I was so excited I could not even sit in one place. I kept pacing up and down the room. An hour-and-a-half later, I was at the airport. I was so nervous with anticipation. Rohan had still not messaged. I was beginning to feel a little sad. In ten minutes, I was about to board and I still had not heard anything from him.

Finally, when I had just sat down in my seat, almost ready for take-off, he called. I answered before the first ring was complete.

"Hello," I said sounding super jumpy.

"Hey, I didn't even hear it ring."

I was a bit embarrassed, "It did ring. The phone was in my hand, so I picked it up immediately."

"Of course," he said.

I could sense his smile in his words.

"So, when do I see you?"

I knew he would not stop asking me that until I was right in front of him. "I'm about to take off real soon."

"Okay. Call me when you land."

"I will."

The flight was perhaps the longest I had ever been on. It seemed like forever. I was extremely restless. I tried to read a book; that didn't really work out. Then I tried watching a movie, which I got bored of within minutes. I even tried to sleep, but no luck. I was just too damn excited.

After what felt like a century, we finally landed. The moment I was allowed to switch my phone on, I did. I was getting frustrated because I was not getting any connectivity. It was when I reached baggage claim that I could see the connectivity bars reaching their maximum. I quickly called Rohan and he answered almost immediately.

"Hey, you're back," he greeted me, sounding more enthusiastic than I had expected.

"Yes, finally," I said sounding equally excited.

"So, what's the plan for tonight?"

"Well, I don't know yet. I will have to figure it out and get back to you."

"Okay, but tell me soon. Okay?"

"I will, as soon as I know."

Before I could even say anything my sister started yelling at me, "Do you mind getting off the phone? You can talk to your lover boy later; our luggage is almost here, and some help would be nice."

I could hear Rohan laugh at the other end.

"Can I call you back?" I asked.

"Sure."

Moments later when we were both in the cab on our way home, my sister asked, "So I guess you told him about your decision to be with him or that you chose him or whatever?"

"Well, I don't know what to call it, but yes, I guess I am with him," I said. I could not help smiling as I said that.

"You *do* know you behave like a crazy, love-sick teenager around Rohan, right? It might be cute for him, but I swear it makes me sick."

I laughed, "I love the feeling. I wish it would never end."

"I'm glad. You made the right decision. What did you say to Jeremy?"

"I called him but he didn't answer; so I messaged saying that we should just be friends, we are better off like that. And he replied saying okay like it didn't matter." I said, still irritated about it.

"I told you he is not worth it. Maybe the time was all wrong. You know sometimes we just meet the right people at the wrong time and it doesn't work out."

PRELUDE TO THE END OF THE YEAR

It was almost evening and I was wondering why Rohan had not called yet. I was looking forward to seeing him it was different now that I had accepted the feelings I had for him. it was getting quite late and I still heard nothing I was beginning to feel a little disheartened and decided to call him up.

He answered almost immediately, "Hi."

"Where are you?" I asked, with a mix of anticipation and annoyance.

He laughed, "Open the door."

For a moment I didn't register.

"I'm outside," he said.

I walked towards the door still on the phone and opened it.

"I wanted to surprise you," he said with a big grin on his face and large pizza box in his hand.

"I was wondering what happened."

"When does your sister get back home?"

"She will be home in about two hours."

"That's enough time for dinner." He said as he walked in and placed the pizza box on the table.

"Want to watch a movie?"

"I'm not sure I have enough time for a movie. We could just sit on the couch and watch some TV"

"Sounds good to me." I said I lay comfortably on the couch and switched on the TV leaving enough space for him to join.

We were watching one of the numerous cooking completion shows. When he said, "I cook an awesome chicken curry."

I laughed, "Really, you know how to cook?"

"Yes, I can cook a number of things actually. I will cook for one day."

I smiled at that thought, though I wasn't sure if and when that would actually happen.

The show had almost ended and we were done with dinner. He still had about half an hour to spare. So we sat and just talked. I told him all about Mumbai and what happened. I could sense him trying to hide a smile.

After a while he had to leave which in a way worked out as my sister arrived moments later. I had not introduced my sister to him yet. I was not ready to. I wanted to when I was sure it was something serious.

Over the next month or so we spend almost all our time together. We watched Nemours movies. Most of the time I choose the movie and he would complain because it would not be a movie he would usually watch but take me for it anyway.

He took me wherever I wanted whether it was a cuisine I wanted to try out or a late night drive to in and out because I was hungry and there was nothing to eat at home.

New Year's was a few days away when he reminded me I had promised to spend it with him. I couldn't wait.

A VERY HAPPY NEW YEAR

For New Year's Rohan gave me the option of three parties. It was only at the last minute that Rohan and I finally decided which of the three party options to go with. We were planning to meet his friends for a quiet in-house kind of party. I had just one hour to get ready and I had absolutely no idea what I was going to wear. My closet was now emptied out onto my bed and I still had nothing to wear. It was freezing cold outside, which made it even more difficult to choose something sexy and warm. To top that, I had the worst cold ever; I could not stop sneezing. I took some super heavy medicine so I didn't spoil any romantic moment that I might have because of my sneezing.

It was almost 11:40 pm when Rohan finally picked me up. I didn't realise it was so late but I was already so dazed because of the medicine, I actually thought I would pass out in the car. I chose to go with warm instead of sexy because I didn't want to fall sick; and ended up dressing plainly. With Rohan, I didn't really have to worry about how I looked. He just wanted to be with me and that's all that really mattered to him. Even in sweatpants I was the prettiest girl to him.

We were running a bit late. When we reached, we hastily rushed down the lobby, towards the lifts. When we reached the floor, right when we reached the door, he grabbed me and kissed me.

"Happy New Year," he said, looking right into my eyes with that look that always made my knees go weak.

I kissed him back "You too," I said.

This was the first time I had ever had anyone to kiss on New Year's and I could not have asked for a more perfect person. I really did love him.

Most of the night was pretty much a blur for me due to my highly medicated state. I was quiet most of the night as I didn't know too many people around. He took care of me made sure I ate something and I was feeling okay and he never left my side. I spent most of my time laying back in the warmth and comfort of his arms.

By about 5:00 am, most people left and soon enough it was just the two of us there. We had the whole room to ourselves and decided to stay.

JUST YOU AND I

Now finally after more than five months we accepted the way we felt about each other. Nothing could have been a better start to the year. I was still a little drowsy, yet I had all the energy in the world to be with him. Somehow having him next to me always made everything better. No matter how sick, sad, or irritated I was, he would make the negativities disappear in no time. All I remembered was him.

That's exactly what he did this time also, when he moved close and kissed me. A kiss that I had been waiting for since the last time our lips last parted. His kisses were always in perfect sync to the mood I was in. His lips felt warm and soft against mine and the cold weather that was giving me goose bumps all this time was replaced by the warmth of the moment. This time neither of us stopped for it was as if his kisses had become my oxygen.

I could feel his cold fingers run down my back so tenderly, so slowly, like droplets of ice cold water which was then followed by a trail of goose bumps. He held me gently in his arms. It was the slowest and sweetest of moments where neither of us had anywhere to go, and time had become inconsequential. I had never felt like this before, I had never wanted to be with someone this much. It scared me. The way I felt for him, it was something I was not sure was in my control. Normally I would never let myself feel like this but with him he made sure I was always comfortable and I felt so safe that the only thing that made sense was to drown in his love.

I became his home; He became my blanket and our hearts a sweet haven. It was surreal.

Moments later, I fell asleep in his arms and my head lay gently upon his chest. He held me close. I could hear his heart beating as if it were my lullaby.

The next morning I woke up in exactly the same position. I had never before all my life woken up in the same position I slept. Not only was I normally a restless sleeper but I also always needed my space. I usually felt suffocated when I didn't get enough space. However, with him I felt suffocated when he was far away from me.

FOR THE FIRST TIME

I was sitting on the couch sipping hot coffee and watching him read the newspaper in his boxer shorts. There was something really sexy about that image. I thought as I laughed to myself. I was just happy that I was with him, finally. I was his and he was mine; just like the way it was meant to be ever since the day we laid eyes on each other or at least I believed so. You could call it fate, if such a thing existed. There was something that felt incredibly natural about being with him.

When he was done with the newspaper, he came and joined me on the couch. I was nervous, afraid I was falling so much in love with him. He sat beside me and I lay my head upon his shoulder and said, "I wish we could just stay here."

"Me too," he said, as he took my hand and held it firmly in his.

We sat there like that, neither of us saying a word. It was so silent, I could hear him breathe. It was then that I had noticed our breathing was in complete harmony. I began drifting into thought again, only to be interrupted, "What're you thinking?" He asked in his usual way.

I smiled and said, "I was just wondering…"

"What?"

"When you first met me, did you ever think that we would end up here, like this?"

He smiled, "Well the day I first met you. I was really busy with work and Karan had called and told me he was with some friends and I should join him. I didn't know who all would be there. I just thought I would go for a while. When we got there, I noticed you and then he introduced us. And you didn't say much or anything at all initially and then we totally hit it off."

"I know, I didn't know you then."

"Uh huh… Every time I looked at you, you would look back at me with this gaze, this slight lingering stare. At first I thought it was better to just ignore it. The second time when you looked at me like that again, it was like you were holding me with your eyes and I felt something. I would not call it attraction or love. In fact, I don't think there is a word in the dictionary that defines how I felt at that moment. Then later Karan told me that you had a guy in your life. I stopped thinking about it then. You really sweet and I just thought that the good ones are always already taken."

I blushed as I heard that he thought I was a good one…well, you know what I mean.

"Can I ask you something else? How come you dropped me home that night? Karan was supposed to drop me home and the next thing I knew, you were."

"Karan suggested I drop you because your house was on the way to mine."

"Oh", I said sounding disappointed.

"What was that for?"

"I thought you dropped me because you wanted to spend time with me."

"I liked the fact that I would get to spend time with you and I wanted to get to know you. But you were seeing someone, so didn't see any point and didn't want to create any complications."

I didn't respond to that.

"I liked the tequila by the way," I said after a brief pause.

"Just so you know I could not get you out of my head, I knew I needed to. I don't know why every time I meet someone nice, they already belong to someone else. You were different. I just could not read you and I always know what someone is thinking. With you, I was just plain curious; I couldn't figure you out. I couldn't help but want to get to know you more."

I was not sure if he said that to make me feel better but it worked. I was about to say something when, I was suddenly interrupted and startled by the sound of his phone ringing. I could make out it was an office call from the way his tone changed to a more assertive and serious one. I knew that meant it was time to leave.

I got up and went to get my coat and bag, and wear my shoes. I put my shoes and was wearing my coat when Rohan walked right over to me without taking his eyes off me for even a second. He looked at me and smiled before he kissed me. He held me really close; his arms wrapped around my waist tightly as he continued to kiss me a little more. I smiled as our lips parted and sunk my head into his chest and hugged him. I slowly moved my lips to his ear and whispered, "I love you".

"I love you too," he said as he pulled me closer and hugged me for a little while longer.

"We should leave now," he said and then kissed me gently on my forehead.

I reluctantly let go of him as we both walked towards the door. Neither of us wanted to leave but we had no choice.

When I got home, I was still dazed. All I could think of was Rohan. I couldn't focus on anything. Last night's events were playing over and over in my head like a broken record. I was lost in thought; I was lost in his love. I think this is what people call being 'love drunk'.

After half an hour of lying there and staring at the ceiling lost in the land of Rohan, I decided to stop thinking about him and text him. "I'm thinking about you. I miss you already. Can't wait to see you again".

He replied back after about ten minutes saying, "Me too".

When I received the message, I had a huge grin on my face. I was about to message him again when I received a second message from him.

"Do you want to meet tonight?"

"What time?" I typed back.

He responded quickly saying, "I don't know, I guess once I'm done with work". I decided it would just be easier to call him. Or maybe it was just an excuse to hear his voice again.

"Hello."

"Hey. So when do I see you tonight?" I asked.

"I'm not sure exactly; after 9 sometime."

"Hmmm..." I said thoughtfully I had known him for long enough to know that when he said sometime after 9, it could mean just about anything.

"I will call you and tell you," he said, sounding a little worried I'd say no.

"Okay." I finally said after quickly thinking it through in my head. I don't know why though because I knew I would end up saying yes, no matter what happened.

"What are you up to anyway?" he asked.

"I was going to sleep," I said feeling a little sad that he had to go directly to work.

"I wish I could also sleep," he said in that cute school boy tone of his.

"I know! I would have loved to cuddle with you and sleep in your arms," I said picturing it in my head. I could almost feel him right there, next to me.

"I would also like that very much," he said.

I felt warm merely by the sound of his voice. "Then just come and join me," I said.

"I wish I could baby," he sounded sad as he said that.

"I know it would be perfect," I said with a huge grin on my face. I had just finished saying that when he said, "Baby, I have to go. Will call you when I leave?"

I hated saying bye to him. "Can I call you when I wake up?"

"Okay. Sure."

"Bye."

"Bye."

I woke up around 9:30 pm and before I even opened my eyes completely, I called him up.

"Hello," he answered.

"Hey, so when do I see you?"

"In about half an hour," he said.

"What?" I had just woken up. "I just woke up; I will have to take a shower and everything."

"Then go quickly."

"Okay, but I may take some time."

"Don't make me wait for too long," he said in that cute voice. It made me giggle.

He laughed and said, "Shut up! I'm twenty minutes away, are you ready?"

"How can I be ready if you don't let me go," I said trying to sound cute.

"Then go."

"I'm going."

"Okay hurry."

"I will try to."

"See you soon."

"Bye."

"Bye."

WHISKEY KISSES

When he reached, I was still not ready. I made him wait for about fifteen minutes while I was touching up my already straightened hair. Then I grabbed my overcoat, put on my boots and ran out the door so fast that I almost tripped over the door mat.

When I got into the car, I kissed him before I even said hello.

"I missed you so much," I said, sounding extremely excited followed by a brief moment of embarrassment for being so forthright.

He responded with a kiss that was so warm, it put me at ease. I loved that he felt the same way about me. Even though he was driving, he kept glancing at me every now and then, making sure I got enough of his attention.

"Are you hungry?" He asked, glancing at me once more.

"Not really. I wouldn't mind just going for a drink though," I responded looking right back into his eyes as his gaze held mine and gave me butterflies in my stomach.

It was this fixated, intense and gentle stare and I could not take my eyes away. He of course had to keep his eyes on the road and couldn't get too distracted. I began to feel a little nervous and started fidgeting with my phone as I stared out at the traffic ahead.

"Can you stop fidgeting so much?"

"I can't help it. I always need something to play with."

"Uh huh," he said, looking at me with one eyebrow raised, and an extremely naughty look in his eyes. "You can play with me," he continued to say in a tone that was a mix of playfulness and shyness.

I smiled as I placed my phone on the dashboard and reached out for his hand on the gear. I liked the way our fingers intertwined and the way he would hold on to my hand, making sure it would not slip out of his.

He slowed down as we approached a red light. He then took my hand and looked at them with this grin on his face and started smiling. I gave him a puzzled look. He then turned to me and said, "You have crooked fingers."

My face fell as he started to chuckle. He noticed that and he took my hand till I felt the touch of his soft lips against it and he kissed each of my crooked fingers gently. Now, that kind of apology I highly approved of.

When we reached our destination and pulled into the parking lot, I didn't want to leave at all. I was happy just where we were as long as I was with him. Nothing else mattered.

His phone rang at that moment, pulling me out of my thoughts. His friends were calling to find out when we were reaching.

"Two minutes," he said.

My heart sank. I was not sure if he could feel my reluctance but he leaned in and kissed me.

Before we knew it, half an hour had passed and we had gotten several calls from his friends wondering what had happened to the two of us. He looked at me and said, "Always making me late."

I laughed, "Well, it was worth it, wasn't it?"

He smiled, "It was."

"You can blame it on me if you like," I said as we got out of the car.

"Idiot," he responded in a soft, affectionate voice as he put his arm around me leading me towards the club where his friends had been waiting for us.

As we walked in, they all kept asking him what had happened to us and why we reached so late. My face turned red and I looked down at the floor hoping no one would notice. After no less than a minute we were at the bar. He held my hand tight and led me through the crowd to make sure I would not get lost.

"You want anything?" He whispered in my ear. His warm breath sent a shiver down my spine.

"No. I'm good for now, maybe one tequila shot or two before we leave."

Rohan being Rohan ordered his signature drink, Chivas with soda and lots and lots of ice along with two tequila shots for the both of us.

While the bartender was getting our drinks, I could feel Rohan's arms slowly wrap around me. He kissed my neck gently determined to bruise me before our drinks reached us. Only to be interrupted by the bartender's hoarse voice informing us that our drinks were ready.

"Tequila now...or...?" I asked looking up at Rohan. I could feel the sharp sting of the hickey he had left of my neck.

"You only wanted it."

"I thought later."

"So you don't want it now?"

"I do. I do. We can't be rude to the tequila."

"You can have more later if you want," he said as he gave me a shot glass filled to the brim with tequila and a lemon wedge with a small amount of salt on it.

"Cheers."

I licked the salt gently before I downed the shot of tequila, which warmed my ears instantly. I calmed my taste buds with the lemon which was followed by further calming on Rohan's part as he kissed me once more.

We then walked toward the dance floor. He had my hand in his and his glass of whiskey in the other. He was not really much of a dancer. However, if there ever was any dancing for him, it always involved him holding me in his arms I had no complaints. I leaned against him, he had his hands around my waist holding me like he never wanted to let go of me. If I moved even a little away, even if by mistake, he'd pull me back towards him, just like he was doing right at that moment.

I loved being close to him and when he kissed me in between

his sips of whiskey. I could taste it in his kiss. I called them 'whiskey kisses'.

We hadn't been there for too long when his friends decided to grab something to eat. Soon after, we were back in the car, on our way to Yellow Brick Road for a very late night dinner.

While everyone was placing their orders, Rohan and I were just looking at each other. The waiter interrupted us by asking us what we wanted to eat.

"You want anything?" Rohan asked me.

"No. I'm not really that hungry. I may have a bite or two from you if that's okay?"

"Sure," he said, as he finished giving the waiter his order.

I was looking around the restaurant at everyone there. It was really crowded for 2:00 am, I thought to myself. I felt a slight kick from under the table. It was Rohan, not looking too happy that I had taken my attention away from him. I couldn't help but smile at his cuteness.

It took about fifteen minutes for the food to arrive and everyone pounced on it like they had not seen food in days.

"You want some?" Rohan asked.

"Only if you give me a bite," I said trying to sound cute but not too sure if that worked.

"I never do the feeding people thing. It is not my thing. So please don't ask me to or expect me to."

My heart sank when he said that; I felt bad. I pretended his comment did not bother me and instead smiled and responded saying, "Well then I don't want anything. Thank you."

Moments later, it was like he had forgotten everything he had just said to me. With his hands, he actually fed me a bite. For a moment I thought he only did that because he was just trying to keep the peace, but he smiled and asked, "Want more?"

I smiled back and nodded.

DRIVING SLOW ON A SUNDAY MORNING

It was 3:00 am on a Sunday morning when we finally said goodbye to all his friends and left. It was just the two of us together again.

It was cold outside and Rohan's hands were freezing. His hands were somehow always cold and mine always warm. I took his hand in mine and warmed it as much as I could, one hand at a time. Before we both got into the car I made sure both his hands were sufficiently warm.

We stayed in the car for a while as it began to rain. I lay my head upon his shoulder gently as I watched the rain drops splatter on the windshield. As I lay there he stroked my hair gently.

"What are you thinking?" he asked.

I laughed, surprised that this was the first time this whole night he asked me that. "Nothing," I responded.

"Will you tell me?"

"There is really nothing to tell."

"So you're keeping things from me now."

"I'm not keeping anything from you." After a brief pause I continued, "I was just thinking that, I like this, just being here with you."

"I like it too," he said and bent down as he kissed me.

. He brought out a side of me that I never knew existed. I felt safe with him. I was myself and not inhibited like I usually am around most people. I was comfortable. Like being with him was the most natural thing in the world. Like this was meant to be. I felt like I was meant to love him like this.

With him I could barely breathe and yet never felt claustrophobic. I forgot that the world existed, and time froze.

The sun was almost up and the rain had stopped. It was now 7:00 am and yet it felt like he picked me up from my house just an hour ago. This is love I guess and I was definitely falling, despite all my efforts not to.

"Shall we go?" He asked, followed with, "It's seven."

"We should, but can we just stop and eat something."

"Sure."

What did I do to deserve someone like this, or maybe I was seeing life through rose-coloured glasses. But who cared! It was my life, my own rose-coloured glasses, and I was happy with it.

It was nearly 8:00 when I finally did reach home, after an almost never-ending goodnight kiss.

JUST A LOVE STORY

When I woke up, I looked at my phone. There was no message from Rohan. I figured he'd be asleep. I sent him a message saying, "I miss last night already" with a sad smiley next to it. I was hoping he would reply to it as soon as he woke up.

I was still feeling quiet lazy and very reluctant to get out from under the sheets. I was tired and sleepy since I had gotten into bed so late. I yelled out to my maid, asking for a steaming cup of coffee. That would surely help me spring out of bed. Okay, spring out is a little too farfetched, maybe stumbling out of bed.

I got my cup of coffee within minutes. After finishing the hot cup of coffee quickly and almost burning my tongue in the hurry, I proceeded to the kitchen to scavenge for some food. After an unsuccessful attempt of finding anything that attracted my palette, I decided to wait for lunch, which according to my maid was going to be served in twenty minutes, perfect amount of time for a quick hot shower.

Later that afternoon while I was lazily lying on the couch watching television after a heavy scrumptious meal, Laksh called. I was feeling a bit lazy to have a conversation but since I had not spoken to him in a while, I answered.

"Hey."

"Hello, what's up?" He asked.

"Nothing much, being lazy and watching re-runs of *Friends* on TV."

"I have not spoken to you in months. How was Mumbai?"

I laughed, "Interesting."

"Yes, that it would have been either way. Could you please elaborate?"

"Well..." I started off by telling him how I had spent time with Jeremy and that it really did seem like things would change, but then he was just being the same. I also told him how I ended up talking to Rohan more than I did with Jeremy even when I was with Jeremy. I told him how my heart just was not in it.

"So then you chose Rohan, I'm guessing?"

"Yes."

"I'm glad. It was about time you let go of him anyway."

I laughed, "I guess."

"What is the doubt?"

"No doubt..."

"I know you too well to fall for your words, Ali. What is it?"

I thought for a moment and then decided to share my thoughts with him. Laksh had always been a good critic of my thoughts and I could trust him, I knew. So I said, "Sometimes I feel that if I stayed with Jeremy I might have actually ended up getting married to him. Don't get me wrong; I'm not saying that I don't love Rohan. I'm crazy about Rohan."

"But...?" he asked.

"Well, Jeremy, like me, wanted to get married at some point and it worked well with my plans. With Rohan, he has no such plans. So I'm not even thinking about it or considering it. I don't know if this thing with Rohan will ever have any future; with Jeremy I knew there would probably be one. If you know what I mean..."

"I do get what you're saying, but Jeremy did not want to commit. So maybe in some years he may or may not have, there was never a guarantee there too. At least Rohan is completely honest with you about his plans. Do you still have feelings for Jeremy?"

"I knew him for two years and feelings like that don't just go away. I'm not saying I love him or anything. I want to be with Rohan, that's for sure. It will take time to fade completely, you know, just the few lingering feelings but nothing romantic or serious just reminiscence of something past."

"Yeah, I get it. But if Rohan is not looking at get married at all, aren't you taking a risk? Didn't you want something with a future?"

"I did, I still do, but I can't help the way I feel. I know it may seem stupid and a waste of time to most people, but I love Rohan and I just can't possibly love anyone else. I'm just not in a place I can feel like that about someone else. I have not been this happy since the first time I fell in love. Laksh, that was like seven years ago. Besides, I don't want to look back and wonder what if or regret not taking the chance. I have this crazy gut feeling about him. He may not be the one but whatever this is, it's meant to happen. The bottom line is I'm happy. Who knows what the future has in store for us; anything is possible."

"I guess if you're happy that's all that matters."

"Exactly! Besides, I have enough experience of protecting my heart. As long as I know and remind myself this might be all that it's ever going to be, I won't get hurt."

"That I am not sure about, but I guess in a way it makes sense."

"Maybe it's not about the whole fairy tale ending. Maybe it's just about the love story. Or maybe we just make our own fairytales." I said smiling to myself at that thought.

"Just be careful whatever you do. I guess that's all I can say. And if he loves you enough, you can talk to him and work these little things out, you know!"

"I will, in good time."

"I'm always here in any case."

I laughed, "Yes, you are."

"Okay, catch you later. Bye."

"Bye."

The moment I hung up, I saw my sister staring right at me.

"What is it?" I asked

"When do I meet him?"

"Meet who?"

"Rohan, who else?"

I thought for a few seconds and said, "Will make a plan and let you know."

"Okay. You better. I shall make my final assessments then."

"I thought you already approved."

"I do. Just have to make sure."

"Okay," I said laughing.

"Good," she said and added, "let me know."

"I will."

"I'm just happy you have someone in your life that makes you happy."

I smiled. He makes me very happy indeed.

DO I SEE YOU TODAY?

I noticed I had about four messages from Rohan between my long phone conversation with Laksh and my sister's request. I couldn't help but smile. The feeling of having the phone blink and knowing it's him always made me happy..

I started typing out a long reply to all his messages but realised it was taking too long so, I decided to call him up.

"Hello."

"Hey, I just saw all your messages."

"Uh huh."

"I was on the phone with Laksh."

"Who is that?" he asked. There was a slight possessiveness in his voice that I liked.

"He is a close friend of mine. I have told you about him before."

"Okay, I don't remember." he said, not sounding too comforted with the thought.

"Okay, so I wanted to ask you something," I said, trying to relax the mood a little.

"What?"

"My sister wants to meet you. Let's meet up tomorrow night. And you're not allowed to say no."

"Okay, let's see. I will figure it out."

"No, let's see is also not an option."

He laughed, "Okay."

After a brief moment of silence, he added, "What do you want to do tomorrow night?"

"Nothing much. Maybe have a few drinks or something."

"Okay," he said in a thoughtful tone.

"So are you busy right now or do you have some time for me?" I asked sounding hopeful.

"I always have time for you."

"I miss you," I said with a grin on my face at his comment.

"Me too..."

"I loved last night," I couldn't hide the happiness in my voice as I said that.

"I loved it too, though we can't do it again okay. I can't get home so late."

I laughed, "I know, neither can I but it was worth it."

"Of course it was baby, totally worth it."

My smile was interrupted with his saying, "I have to get back to work now, will ping you okay."

"Okay," I said in a low sad voice.

I was just about to say bye and hang up, when he said, "So, do I see you today?"

Those five words were my favourite. "I could," I said.

"Will try and come there and see you for about half an hour."

"Okay,"

"Will call you and tell you. Bye."

"Bye."

I loved that all my conversations with him ended with a big grin on my face.

I knocked on my sister's door. She didn't respond, which was so typical of her. I'm sure she had her headphones on with music blasting so loud that she was oblivious to everything around her.

"Alisha," I yelled, but no response.

I dialled her number, knowing that her phone was one thing that never felt her sight. It barely even rang when her door flew open.

"What was the call for?" she asked.

"I knocked several times; you didn't respond. Calling you up was easier."

She gave me a funny look with one brow raised.

"Stop giving me looks. I wanted to tell you that we are going out tomorrow night."

"Rohan?" she asked with a teasing look.

"Yes." I answered trying to keep a straight face, but her almost never ending stare with that annoying smirk got the better of me and I smiled.

My sister decided to be a bitch and started laughing at me. I blushed as I left her room and shut the door behind me.

MY LITTLE IDIOT

Rohan finally called after what felt like ages.

"Hello," I answered attempting to control my excitement.

"I'm leaving work now. Can we meet?"

Can I? I thought. I would love to! I settled with a, "Yes, I can. When?"

"Twenty minutes."

"Okay," I said.

"Great, see you then."

"Okay."

"Bye."

"Bye."

This time I was showered and ready before he even called. I decided to watch some television while I waited for him. I know he said twenty minutes, but I could not help but look at my phone wondering if I had missed his call telling me he was waiting outside. That's another one of my favourite words, 'outside'.

And soon enough my phone beeped showing off an SMS from Rohan with the magical word 'outside'.

Once I was in the car, he looked over at me and said, "All ready?"

I laughed, "Yes, this time I was ready and waiting."

"So where do you want to go?"

"Well I'm kind of hungry."

"Me too," after a pause he added, "what do you want to eat?"

"How about we grab some pizza?"

"Pizza sounds good. And where?" he asked.

"Dominos," I said with a huge grin on my face. I just absolutely loved their garlic bread sticks.

"You have any other preference?" I asked.

"No, I'm good. I also like Dominos."

I swear it seemed a match made in heaven, I girlishly thought to myself, while we headed down to the closest Dominos outlet. I decided to reconfirm our plans for the next night.

"You sure about tomorrow night… my sister really wants to meet you."

"Yes, I'm sure." he said followed with a, "What have you told her, that she really wants to meet me?"

He had this inquisitive look in his eyes, much like children do when they discover something new and they are trying to figure out what it is. He reminded me of a little boy at times. And I liked that because it made me feel like he needed me to take care of him. I liked being needed.

"So?" he asked interrupting my thoughts.

"I have told her a lot about you."

This statement aroused his curiosity even more than before.

"What all have you told her?" He asked, sounding a tad bit nervous.

"Just how we met and everything," I said nervously.

"What is everything?"

"Well, when I was in Mumbai trying to figure everything out, she helped. She even read some of your messages to me and kept calling me crazy because apparently it was evident that you're the one I should be with." I said finally stopping to catch my breath.

"What was so evident?"

"Since when do you ask so many questions? That is my job." I said looking at him a little surprised, since I was not used to him asking so much.

"Why? You have a problem if I ask you questions? Are you keeping things from me?" He asked me in a half joking, half serious manner.

"No. Just not used to it. And for the record, you can always ask me anything."

"Then tell me what's so evident?"

"Well, for starts, while I was there I chatted more with you than with Jeremy. Then the type of conversation I had with Jeremy was very general. You kept messaging me and Jeremy didn't even bother to reply to my one message."

He looked at me with the questioning look in his eyes and I knew my answer did not satisfy him.

"Well, you missed me and Jeremy was just kind of cold."

"Uh huh," he said, still not convinced.

"You're nicer to me," I said. I could feel my whole face turn red and I had no idea where to look. I could see him smiling from the corner of my eye and it just made my face turn redder.

"So, what exactly did she say to you?"

"That I was being an idiot and it was very obvious that you liked me and paid more attention to me than Jeremy did. She also said that Jeremy took me for granted and I'd be happier with you because you seemed to want to be with me."

I swear at that moment I thought I saw him blush a little. His silence and refusal to make eye contact confirmed my suspicion.

After a brief moment of silence he said in a very matter of fact manner, "I do want you."

I smiled, "I want you too."

We finally reached our destination. We were both so hungry that we ate our food in almost complete silence. I ended up eating so much that I couldn't even get up.

"I think I ate too much." I said as we walked towards the car.

"Me too."

"Do you need to get back?"

"Why? What do you have in mind?"

"Just don't want to go home yet," I said sadly.

"When do you?" He asked.

"Why would I want to when I'm with you?" I asked trying not to sound too cheesy.

I thought he would laugh at that, but instead he just kissed me. His soft lips on my cheek warmed me up and felt perfect on such a cold winter evening.

"Idiot" he said softly and added, "So what do you want to do?"

"Some more of this," I said, as I pulled him close to me and returned his kiss.

"You know, I could do this forever." He said in a soft whisper and smiled.

"Can I ask you something?" I said, my tone was much more serious this time.

"Yes…"

"What if this all goes away?" I asked as I sat up straighter in my car seat.

He took my hand in his and in an almost completely serious tone asked me, "And where will it go?"

I could not help but laugh. He always tried to make things sound so simple and happy. "You know, this kind of stuff lasts for a few months and then everything changes."

"What changes?"

"Feelings change. What if you get bored of me or you stop loving me?"

He put his arms around me and held me close and said these four words that put me to rest. "I'm not going anywhere."

"So, you're mine to keep then?" I asked sounding a little disbelieving.

"I'm all yours, my love."

"Don't go anywhere, okay? And stay mine always."

"I'm yours only. I don't know why you have to think so much."

"I can't help it, I really do try not to but I'm like that."

"I know you're my little idiot and I love my little idiot."

I blushed. "I love you too."

CAN'T STOP THIS THING WE STARTED

I woke up with the same pleasant feeling I had been waking up with for the last few days. I was a little surprised, to be honest, I was so sure the feeling would have maybe dwindled down a little by now, but it still felt like the first day our eyes met. I knew for sure if he kept looking at me like he did the first night, I would keep falling for him a little more each time. I knew I could not afford to fall for him like this; I had to save myself from going totally bonkers. I needed to control this.

Everything was happening faster than I planned; my world was spinning at a speed I couldn't fathom. Despite my best efforts to control it getting so serious so fast, I would forget everything when I was with him and would just be myself. I loved it, no doubt, and also felt safe with him, like I could trust him to keep my heart safe.

I smiled to myself at the thought and rolled over and went to sleep again, hoping I would meet Rohan somewhere in my dreams again.

It was about four hours later when I felt a cold wind against my body. I sleepily looked for my sheet and ended up in a tug of war with my sister.

"Get up you lazy bum. It's nearly lunch time."

I mumbled something even I didn't understand as I slowly dragged my feet to the bathroom.

About twenty minutes later I yelled out, "Alisha".

"Yes, what is it?" she asked sounding grumpy.

"Why are you so grumpy?"

"I will tell you about it during lunch… what do you need?"

"Can I get a towel, please?"

She came back and chucked my red towel on my face and went to back to frantically messaging someone on her phone.

When I was finally ready and the both of us were at the lunch table waiting for the food to be served, I snatched her phone from her hand and demanded an answer to my question.

"What's going on?"

"College drama. I'm so fucking pissed off."

"I'm sure it will be fine. Cheer up and don't forget we are going out tonight. How does that sound?"

She smiled, "I finally meet prince charming, would not miss it for the world. Well, your prince charming, lest you go all possessive."

I laughed.

I quickly messaged Rohan to make sure he remembered. "Yes baby, I do remember. Let me know if you want me to pick you guys up, ok". I sent him a smiley saying, "will do baby, love you".

"Love you too," he replied almost immediately.

"Your love affair is making me sick," Alisha said.

"Thanks," I said half meaning it, half sarcastic.

"Alisha?"

"Yes? Why the serious tone?"

"Do you think he is worth it?"

"Why? Don't tell me you are thinking of running already?"

"No, not at all... I don't really think I would ever want to." I said as I watched Alisha's expression change. She seemed a bit surprised.

"You're falling for him. Well It's about time you have been together long enough." She said as she picked up our dirty plates and walked towards the kitchen.

"But do you think he is worth it?"

"Honestly, I don't know. I can't answer that but what I do know is that *you* think he is worth it. Otherwise you would not be falling for him like this. I know he cares about you. I know that when you were sick a few weeks ago he came over when I wasn't there with a bag full of medicines and took care of you. He tells you he loves you almost every single day. And that time you were upset with him about something, you didn't tell me what but I remember that he spoke to you for hours at some crazy time in the wee hours of the morning and he only hung up once you were all comfortable and secure again."

"How do you know all this?"

"The walls are thin so I can hear some of your conversations when you think I can't. Most importantly I know you really care about him because you do want me to meet him."

I smiled as she finished her sentence and walked towards my room while I thought about what she had just said.

MEETING MY PRINCE CHARMING

It was almost 8:30pm, Alisha and I decided to take the metro and meet Rohan and Karan at Route 04.

"Why do you look so nervous?" Alisha asked.

"The thing you said about me wanting you to meet him. Do you realize that I have never introduced you to anyone I have ever dated before?"

"What about…" she said followed with a long pause, "Actually that is true. When you think about it, this is actually the first time you have thought of introducing me to anyone. I think it's because this is the first time in years that you have cared for anyone so much and consider him to be special enough. I think you know that this is going to be something more than usual, something extra special." She said with a wink.

I was a little embarrassed when she said that and a little scared because I guess I was still getting used to feeling like this. "I know and I'm happy. I'm not used to it," I responded.

"Not used to what?"

"Used to having someone love me so much and feeling this way so strongly about someone," I said as I blushed, hoping she would not notice and start teasing me about it.

"Oh Please! You have lots of people who would practically do anything for you. You just never give them a chance. Fuck that, you don't even give them a glance." She said as she started laughing at her own joke.

"It's not like that. You make me sound like some mean heartbreaker. There has just never been a connection. Like that heart skipping a beat and going weak in the knees feeling."

"The problem, my darling sister, is that you are extremely

choosy and you're looking for a fairy tale in your life story. Fairytales don't exist. You're just lucky you found someone like Rohan."

"And what's so wrong with believing in fairytales?" I asked, as we walked out the train towards the exit.

"There isn't anything wrong with that. I just want to see you happy and I don't want to see you get disappointed, and when you believe in something that doesn't exist it only leads in disappointment." she said as she hugged me.

I didn't say anything I knew she was right but I still couldn't help believing there had to be some truth in fairytales.

A few seconds later my phone rang. It was Rohan calling, "Hello."

"Where are you?"

"Almost there."

"Karan and I are sitting upstairs, okay."

"Yes, will see you soon. Don't miss me too much."

"Baby, I will keep missing you till you get here."

I had a big grin on my face as he said that. He always said the sweetest things, like he rehearsed it or something. He always knew exactly what I wanted to hear and exactly what needed to be said to put a smile on my face.

"Okay, so which floor did he say they were on," Alisha asked as we walked up the stairs of Route.

"Keep walking, second floor."

He was right there sitting at the table near the stairs. I had a big smile on my face as I walked towards him and put my arms around him and kissed him gently on his cheek. He hugged me tight like he had not seen me in over a week.

"Hi, I'm Alisha," she said, introducing herself to Karan.

"I'm Karan."

"My sister is kind of rude, so had to introduce myself."

"I know, she is pathetic."

I heard the drama going on behind my back and quickly put in, "I'm not pathetic". "Alisha, meet Rohan. Rohan, this is my sister Alisha."

"Hi," said Rohan, still holding on to me.

"Hi, nice to finally meet you. This girl here can't stop talking about you."

"That is not true," I said only to be completely ignored.

However, a minute later Rohan whispered in my ear, "So what did you tell her that was not true?"

"So you heard when I said that?"

"I always hear what you say, baby," he said as he kissed me on my cheek.

"Idiot," I said as I turned towards him and smiled.

I could see Alisha watch us from the corner of her eye and smile. I knew she approved of him.

A little while later, Karan left and then there was just the three of us.

"So Rohan, I heard you met the boy you stole her away from," Alisha said.

"Yes."

"How was that night?"

"I was actually not planning to go out that night at all. Why would I want to go when she had her guy and all?"

"Then why did you change your mind?" I asked him.

Right then Alisha got up, "I'm going to get myself another drink while you two finish this conversation."

We both didn't even realize and just continued talking.

"So? I didn't know you were not going to come."

"I was not planning to. Then Karan called me up and he was like, 'dude what's happening? What's going on with you and Aleah?' and I said nothing is going on. Why do you ask? Then he said she was asking about you. I asked what you were asking about me and he said you wanted to know if I was coming to TC that night, and that you told him to make sure I would."

"Well ya, he told me he called you and I hadn't seen you since so I did want to see you again."

"I know. I didn't expect that you would want to see me again but since you had asked him I thought maybe I would go and see what happens."

"Okay."

"You know, that day I actually went home and shaved for you."

"What do you mean?"

"I don't know. I just thought you would like me better all clean shaven." He said this with a slight hint of embarrassment.

I smiled and held his hand hoping to make him feel comfortable.

"So, I see everything is fine." Alisha said as he joined us back at the table.

Rohan laughed.

"So the answer to your question… I didn't really interact with him much."

"Of course, you didn't. You were so busy trying to get hold of her attention."

"When we got a table and sat down, I quickly sat next to her. After that, everything just happened like fate took over or something."

"And how exactly did that work?" she asked smiling.

"Well, she came to leave her bags in my car and I had a bottle in my car and she seemed upset with Jeremy and the two of us talked and shared the tequila. It was just so easy to have a conversation with her, it felt natural. It really did not feel like it was the second time we were meeting. It felt like we had known each other for a while."

"You just left Jeremy there," she said looking right at me.

"It was not that long, like a few minutes and he was totally ignoring me and just being weird for some reason." I said followed by, "It's not like he was bothered. He didn't seem to care. He should have been jealous or at least protective like she is mine kinds but he just didn't care." I looked over at Rohan hoping he would add something more.

"Well, she did tell him she was going with me and would be back in a while. He just nodded like it was all cool. If I was him,

I wouldn't have let her out of my sight."

I blushed when he said that and my sister just smiled in acknowledgement.

About three hours later, Alisha hinted at going home, alone. "I think I will head out too, and leave you love birds alone."

"We can drop you." Rohan said.

"You sure you don't want to carry on?"

"Yes, it's cool. Let's go." He said as he finished paying the bill.

I got up and he slid his arm gently around my waist and escorted me down the stairs like a true gentleman.

After we dropped Alisha off home, we decided to go for a short drive. I turned the stereo on loud to 'Iris by the Goo Goo Dolls' because we both of us loved that song. I turned it up and attempted to sing but realised it was too soon in the relationship for him to know I could not sing to save my life.

He gave me a look.

"What's the look for?"

"Were you singing?"

"I considered it but decided not to."

"Why is that?"

"Because you would leave me if you heard me sing."

He started to laugh, "I know you can't sing well, but that's not reason enough for me to leave you."

"Then what is?" I asked, in a more serious tone.

"I love everything about you," he said flashing me the most irresistible smile ever as he reached out for my hand.

"I love you, Rohan" I said as I laughed at him being all adorable.

"You know I was glad you took my hoodie that day. I was really drawn to you for some reason. I just wanted an excuse to see you again. I knew you were seeing someone, but I just knew that I wanted you in my life even if it was just as a friend. I enjoyed just talking to you. I just wanted to get to know you better. In fact, the day after we met that time I told my sister about you."

"Okay, what did you tell her?"

"I was in bed, not feeling like getting out and was thinking about you. I was lost in thoughts of you when my sister came in to wake me up. She asked me what I was thinking so I told her that I met a girl some time back who is Karan's friend and really nice."

"And...?"

"And that I really really liked her and we totally got a long but she was with someone else, and I didn't know what to do about it."

"Okay... You told your sister all this and kept telling me to fix things up with Jeremy. What if it had worked out with him?" I asked curious to know what he would say.

"Obviously I couldn't tell you to leave him and be with me. Besides we were just getting to know each other and it was important to me that I had you in my life as a friend."

"So you did kind of want to be with me then?"

"Yes idiot. Why what did you think?"

"I don't know."

"Uh huh..."

"So anyway what did your sister say?" I asked.

"She asked me if I was sure that I really liked you. I told her that there was definitely something about you. Then she said, if it's meant to be, it will happen and I should not think about it so much and just be there. I told her that you had been having issues with your guy and I had been telling you to fix things with him."

"What did she say to that?"

"She said don't do anything. Just let it be and see what happens. I did like you but I didn't really want to come between two people. So I agreed with her."

"Okay."

"She told me I would fall for you."

"Was she right?" I asked a little nervously.

"Yes."

"You should have told me that you wanted to be with me."

"I tried to, in my own way."

I smiled and kissed him.

"I should get home before Alisha falls asleep and I get locked out." And then added with a naughty smile, "But just between the two of us I don't really want to go."

"I know baby, neither do I. But we have to," he said with a sad face as he turned the car around and headed home to drop me.

I had no idea how I ended up with someone so perfect. How could I not believe in fairy tales when I had someone like him by my side? We kissed good night and I reluctantly got out of the car.

"Call me once you're home," I said.

"I will call from the landline number; my phone battery is almost dead."

"Okay baby," I said as I waved goodbye.

About an hour had passed and he still had not called. I was wondering what was wrong and if he got home alright when I received as message from him saying, "I can't get through from the landline. Love you baby, I'm going to dream of you here in my arms."

I would have cursed the phone network company if his message had not made so happy.. I couldn't help but smile; he really was adorable. "Goodnight my love. Can't wait to see you in my dreams," I replied.

I tucked myself into bed, closed my eyes and drifted into dream land hoping I would meet him there just like he suggested.

THE APPROVAL

The next morning when I woke up, I was surprised to see my coffee ready and waiting for me at the dining table. I looked around and saw my sister walk towards me with a huge grin on her face.

"What's going on?"

"I approve of him."

I laughed, "That's what this is about?"

"He seems really nice and it's so obvious that he is into you and loves you. It's so cute. So I'm doing my sisterly duty of letting you know I approve. So let me know when the wedding bells start to ring. "

I smiled.

"I wish I had a guy who looked at me the way he looks at you." She said imitating an agitated lover's sigh. She giggled a bit and added, "You know what I mean, right? But I'm still surprised you were confused about it."

"Under the circumstances, it was only fair for me to give Jeremy a chance."

"True, and you made the right decision."

"He is kind of perfect, isn't he?" I flashed a smile as big as I could.

"Well I'm not really one of those crazy romantic people like you, but he is. Just be careful. You told me he isn't looking for anything serious and you seem so deeply into it. I don't want you to get hurt."

"I know, and I have thought about that. But I'm so happy. I realise that it might not take me anywhere in terms of a secure future, but I love him and it's so worth it. It's going to hurt all the same in the end, right? I'm happy right now and I would rather be crazy in love and happy for a few years than look back and wonder."

"That's the girl I once knew. You used to be so hopelessly romantic and then you just became so cynical. I miss this annoying side of you at times. You have changed a lot since you met him."

I gave her a slight sceptical look.

"In a good way, I mean. There are some couples who bring out the worst in each other and others who bring out the best in each other."

"I like the sound of that."

"Crazy girl, I have to go for now. Will see you later."

She was out of the room in a flash, leaving me to think about what she had just said. I was so happy that Alisha had approved of Rohan and couldn't wait to tell Rohan. I was sure he wanted to know what she had thought of him. I called him up immediately, but he didn't answer. I was just about to hang up when he finally answered with a sleepy hello.

"I woke you up. I'm sorry. I can call back later."

"It's fine. I love waking up to your voice. Come here, baby, to me."

"Are you sure?"

"Yes. I want you."

"Okay. I will be there soon."

"Really?"

"Are you having second thoughts about the invitation?" I teased him.

"No, come soon."

"Okay going for a shower and will be there in no time."

The inevitable grin was back to my face as I ran to take a shower.

YOUR LOVE IS MY ANCHOR

I knocked at his door and called out, "Hey, I'm here."

His still sleepy voice was faint behind the door, "The door is open. And come straight to my room."

"Okay." I walked into his room and saw him still in bed.

"Are you going to get out of bed and kiss me?"

He didn't say anything, rather pulled me into bed with him. I started laughing.

"Wait, let me get my shoes off."

"Only your shoes?"

"What will you do then?"

"Come here and I'll show you" he said, grabbing me again, and started tickling me till I couldn't breathe.

"Okay, stop, please," I protested. I hated being tickled. He knew that, but always did that on purpose to hear me laugh and make fun of me.

He laughed as I looked at him with pleading puppy dog eyes.

"Okay, come here," he said pulling me close to him and wrapping his arms around me. I liked it so much.

"You smell nice," he said as his breath tickled me a little.

"Don't I always?" I tried to stay calm and in control.

"Yes, but you taste better." He said with a really naughty grin on his face.

I ran my fingers down his chest. He grabbed my hands and held me hostage.

"Don't scratch me. I already have scars, so many of them."

"That's not my fault," I responded, attempting to sound innocent.

"Then whose fault is it?"

"Yours," I said laughing

"Uh huh..." he said and pulled me closer and stared to kiss me.

I loved being painted with his love. It reminded me of New Year's Eve and the moments when we lay beside each other forgetting the meaning of time.

I just loved being like this with him like nothing else mattered but us. His toes tickling mine, his teasing my on purpose and making me feel things I never knew possible. He was always so careful with me. He knew exactly what I liked and wanted and exactly how to make me feel. He soft whispers and gentle touch were always so full of love. It's a nice feeling to just lay back in the arms of someone you love and forget all your troubles.

"I love this. Can't we just be like this always?" I could hardly speak.

He laughed and kissed me. "You're mine, okay. The whole of you is mine; these lips are only for me to kiss."

I laughed, "Only for you. Your love is my love baby."

As I moved away, I almost fell off the bed and he quickly pulled me back into his arms.

I looked at him with a pretend shocked expression on my face, "I almost fell off the bed!"

He laughed, "But you didn't. I'm here to look out for you," he said and kissed me again.

"And who looks out for you?"

"I have someone higher up."

"How do you know he didn't send me into your life to do the same and take care of you and to love you? Because I think he planned it."

"It was the other way around I was the one he sent, idiot." He smiled an adorable smile at that.

"Then what was I sent into your life for... decoration?"

"For loving me, taking care of me and being my emotional support and for being my home."

"That's what I just said. And I don't want to lose you, ever."

"Neither do I. I will hold you tight; won't let go. You have my heart."

"I promise I will always take care of it."

"I don't deserve so much goodness in my life. It always comes for a while and goes away. I have always been disappointed in life. You are one person who I can put next to my parents and say as I hope I don't disappoint them. I hope I don't disappoint you."

"I love you." I was teary-eyed when he said this with such love and tenderness.

"I love you too," he said, almost instantly.

As he kissed me on my forehead, I told him, "Now hurry up and get out of bed and go shower."

"Will you join me?"

"I would have, but I don't want to mess up my hair."

"Idiot, you and your excuses." he said as he tumbled out of bed.

BOYFRIEND

Numerous months had passed, but nothing seemed to have changed. Sometimes it felt like I had just met him; at other times it felt like I had known him all my life. All through my life, I had not found anyone who interested me this much or could hold me with his heart. It usually always faded away before it even started. With him, everything was different from the start, and I loved being with him.

Everything just happened so fast, neither of us could keep up. From being friends or maybe like trying to be friends, to kissing, to not being able to stay away from each other we finally ended up dating. Neither of us thought it would ever get more serious than that but, somehow now was way more than all of that, he was my boyfriend and my best friend.

When we started off, we weren't thinking about being in a relationship. I'm not even sure when things started changing and made me fall in love with him. I didn't want to just date him or be another girl to him; I wanted more, I wanted to mean everything to him and now I did.

It had happened so naturally, like it was meant to happen. It wasn't like we had to think of what the next step should be. His being my boyfriend made life a better place to live in.

The best thing was, we never lost our friendship. That was the one thing that brought us together. We just understood each other and emotionally connected. Somehow when it came to each other's feelings we both understood each other and knew exactly how the other person felt or would feel. We had both opened our hearts to each other and become so vulnerable with each other that we both knew each other's strengths and weakness. We knew each other enough to know what would hurt the other but we trusted each other even more. We were always there for each other.

It was like he gave me a part of his heart in exchange for a part of mine and in time we became so enmeshed in each other that the parts got so integrated within us it was inseparable and irreversible. And no matter what happens there would always be a part of one in the other's hearts.

OUT OF SIGHT, OUT OF MIND

It was nearing time for Rohan's birthday and I was as excited as I was nervous. I wanted to get him something special and was trying to think of ways to make it special for him. He was very particular about things he bought for himself and I didn't want to goof up. So I decided to just call him and ask him.

"Hello"

"Hey baby, were you busy?"

"Yes a bit, I was just making my holiday plans with Karan."

"Holiday plans? Where to…?"

"Singapore"

"So you will be away from me?"

"Not for too long baby."

"But you're going without me," I said sadly.

"Would you come with me?" He asked teasingly.

"I can't."

"Idiot," he said in his cute little boy voice.

"You idiot! Leaving me behind," I tried sounding cute.

"I will be back soon baby." His voice was consoling but I was tempted to tease him.

"But what if you go and forget about me or something."

"Would you ever let me forget you?" He asked, trying to act smart.

"Very funny," I said sounding like a grumpy five-year-old.

"If I was in front of you, I'd have kissed you to shut you up."

"But you're not here."

"Just wait and watch what happens when I see you."

I could feel his smile all the way across the phone line and it made me laugh.

"Just don't leave me okay."

"I'm not going anywhere baby, I'm happy with you. You're all mine."

"I maybe all yours, but the question is… are you all mine?'

"I am yours."

"You sure…?"

"Yes, of course I'm sure, idiot."

"Okay."

"What did you call for?"

"Oh that. I wanted to know what you wanted for your birthday."

"You."

"That you have anyway, birthday or no birthday," I said smiling, "but what do you want as a present?"

"Just you, wrapped up."

I realised this was going to be an endless and hopeless conversation. "Okay, never mind. Go back to your holiday planning, idiot."

"You idiot!"

I just laughed and said, "Bye."

"Hey wait," he said just when I was about to cut the call.

"What?"

"When am I seeing you again?"

"How does tomorrow sound…?"

"So far away," he said sadly.

"Baby today is almost over. It's less than twenty-four hours."

"Okay. Miss me till then."

"I will. You also miss me," I said with a smile.

"I always do," he said in the most adorable voice ever.

I laughed, "Bye baby."

"Bye."

I know he was trying his best to make sure I was comfortable being without him in the country for a few days. We had never really been apart like this before. You know what they say about out of sight out of mind. Well, I was in no mood to test that theory.

YOU'RE MY FAVOURATE HABIT

I seemed to have developed a new habit over the last few days, and an addictive one at that. Calling Rohan up before I went to sleep was something my day felt incomplete without. These goodnight calls to him were my daily routine. I knew it was a dangerous thing to do, to get this close to someone, but I just could not help it. And it seemed too late to stop.

This time also, I called him once I was all comfortably tucked into bed.

"Hello."

"Hey."

"What you doing?" he asked.

"Was just about to sleep, called to say goodnight. I missed you today."

"I missed you too."

"So did you figure out your holiday plan?"

"Not yet."

"Can you please just be here on your birthday? If you don't spend your birthday with me, I'm not going to talk to you." I was a little surprised for the way I said it to him; I was planning to go for a more casual approach and just check if he would be here or not. Worry about his reaction engulfed me in that moment, but he just laughed.

"I will be back before my birthday."

"Promise?" The excitement in my voice couldn't be missed.

"Promise"

"Okay," I said feeling a little better.

"Don't think so much; go sleep now baby."

"Okay, goodnight."

"Goodnight."
"I love you, Ali."
"I love you too."
"Bye."
"Bye."

WISH YOU DIDN'T HAVE TO GO

That evening, after a slightly busy day at work, I went to meet Karan and Rohan at Route. When I got there, both of them were already there, sipping on their respective mugs of beer. After I greeted them and sat down, Karan started talking about their holiday. Just then, Rohan whispered in my ear, "We decided to go day after tomorrow and I will be back in a week, which is before my birthday."

"I wish you didn't have to go."

"I know baby. I will come back soon."

"Don't forget about me," I said, trying to maintain the puppy face expression.

"Of course, I won't. You're mine."

I was feeling better when he said that; he always knew how to make me smile.

"Meet me again before you leave, just me!"

"Tomorrow night I will, just us."

"Okay."

I was already getting impatient for tomorrow evening to get here. The next evening seemed very far away. I don't know how I managed to get through a whole day of work with Rohan so strongly on my mind. I was thinking of giving him something to remember me by, so he'd miss me while he was away. I told him to come home that evening after work. I had just finished dinner when he arrived. I was on the couch watching television when he walked in and slid right next to me, wrapping his arms tightly around me. I placed my head in that little nook right near his shoulder, which I felt was meant for that purpose alone. He kissed my forehead and I smiled because I loved him doing that.

"I missed you." I said as I put my arms around his.

"I missed you too baby."

I moved my head towards him and gently kissed him. I loved the feeling of his warm lips against mine as he kissed me back. I lay there, my arms firmly wrapped around his neck. It felt like I had the whole world in my arms.

"You're mine, don't forget that."

"You don't forget that." He said, all of a sudden.

"I'm not the one going so far off and for so long," I said in mock anger.

"But I'm leaving you here without me. Then how will you be protected from all the men trying to steal you." He said sounding so adorably cute. How could I ever doubt his love for me?

"Nobody is trying to steal me from you, idiot." I said as I kissed him yet again.

His wrapped his hands around me tighter. That reminded me yet again that I didn't want him to go. He had his flight in a few hours. I just wanted to be with him till he had to leave.

He was raining kisses all over me when he suddenly stopped to look at me and said, "What're you thinking?"

"I love feeling you this close to me," I said with my eyes lost in him.

He laughed, "Baby, you're my home now."

"You better always only come home, no checking in anywhere else." I said sternly.

He laughed. "There is nowhere else I want to be," he said as he kissed me softly.

"Miss me, okay" I said sadly, more as a request than a command.

"I will."

"What time do you leave?"

"In a few hours…"

"Then shouldn't you get ready?"

"I know, but I don't feel like leaving you. I like holding you in my arms," he said as he pulled me closer and held me so tight I could barely breathe.

Fifteen minutes later, I had I helped him gather his things as he got ready. It was time now. I hated goodbyes even if they were not forever.

"I will message you from the airport. Okay?" he said as he kissed me on my forehead.

"Okay," I responded as I walked him to the door.

Just when I was about to shut the door, he pushed it back open, grabbed me and kissed me.

As our lips parted, I felt his intense look on me and asked, "What? Why are you looking at me like that?"

"The first time I kissed you, my heart was racing so fast. This may sound like a movie line, but I swear I had butterflies in my stomach. It was like I was kissing someone for the first time."

I blushed.

"Miss me," he said.

"I already do," I said as I sadly watched him disappear into the darkness of the night.

ONE VERY LONG WEEK

He kept his promise and messaged me from the airport saying, "I love you baby, stay mine until I'm back", followed with five kisses. I smiled and responded, "Of course baby, you miss me too, and come back soon".

The week passed by so slowly. I kept myself busy trying to figure what to get him for his birthday. I consulted his friends and Alisha, and tried whatever I could. Finally I settled for something that I was hoping would mean something to him.

I spent hours going through all his friends' albums on Facebook, his pictures wherever I could find them, and finally gathered a few nice pictures to get a collage made. Plus I really wanted to frame it so he could hang it up on his wall and remember me every time he looked at it. I put pictures of him alone and those with his friends and just one with me. I didn't want it to be a mushy thing.

I know it was not a very unique idea but it meant something. I was really hoping none of his ex-girlfriends had done something like this before, because I wanted to make it special. It also kept me busy for the whole week. The day before he got back, I collected it from the shop. It was heavier than I had imagined, but I liked it. I just hoped he would like it too.

When I got home that evening, the first thing I did was show it to Alisha.

"So what do you think?"

"I think it's perfect. He will definitely like it and he'd notice that should you've put in a lot of effort."

"I hope he does. I can't wait for him to see it."

She laughed, "Knowing you, you might just give it to him before his birthday."

"Very funny. I won't and also, I thought maybe I could leave it with you for safe keeping."

"Sure."

She took the whole frame and she was carrying it to her room she said, "You really are in love with him, aren't you?"

I stayed quiet for a while and then in a low whisper I said, "Yes". I knew she had not heard me.

When she came back to my room, she placed herself comfortably on my bed and asked me again. "You're in love with him, aren't you?"

Every time she asked me that, my heart would beat faster.

"You can't deny it, you know. I can hear you crying through the walls before you sleep and you chanted "I miss him" so many times that I don't remember you saying anything else to me throughout this week."

I felt a little embarrassed that she'd heard me crying, even though it was like the one time. But she was right about one thing, I was in love with him for sure.

"Yes, I am in love with him."

She smiled as she got up and left my room, but just as she was about to shut the door she said, "I'm happy for you. Just don't get hurt. I know it's not easy for you to give your heart to somebody, like this."

I smiled, "Thank you."

I was also happy for me and a little scared too. This one week made me realise even more how much I loved him and how I really felt about him and how important he really was to me. I knew I was completely in love with him; I just didn't realise I was far into him and there was no looking back now. I was not really ready to accept the depth and seriousness of my feelings for him. But somehow, knowing he loved me back, gave me the courage to just keep on loving him, and to be his completely, no holding back.

I was just hoping when he got back, he would feel the same way. The out of sight out of mind thing really scared me.

WITH YOU

I can't stop thinking about you
I keep craving more
The more I think about how much I love you
The more I know
I don't ever want to stop
It's the comfort I feel when I'm around you
It's the assurance in your eyes
It's the way I know I couldn't love anyone
The way I love you
I lose sense of all things practical
I get mesmerised in your presence
With a single touch you can make me feel
Things that I have perhaps
Never felt before
You make me forget everything around me
It's like all there is
Is 'us'
You have me in the palm of your hand
My heart is in your heart
You're all I know now
Your world is my world
I have nowhere else to go
I don't care about protecting my heart anymore
I'd rather dream
Of being with you
My days are empty when you're not there
Only I know the urgency I feel
When I don't see you
I remember clearly the first day we met
I looked into your eyes and
Never found my way out
I have never been the type to stay so long
But,
You hold me with your eyes

And you keep me with your heart
And there is nowhere else
I'd rather be
But in this love story
WITH YOU.

OF HOMECOMING

I knew he was flying back that night and sleep evaded me. I kept waking up to see if he had left a message. Finally, on maybe what was the nth time, I saw a message from him saying, "I missed you baby, lots. See me soon, okay, I need you time". I was extremely happy and completely wide awake after reading that, so much for a good night's sleep.

I quickly replied, "I need time you time too, and lots of it. I missed you more than you would ever know."

He was quick in asking, "Can I see you today?"

My heart fell a little as I texted back, "I can't see you today; one of my aunts is in town and coming over for dinner. Maybe tomorrow please?'

He didn't reply for a while and I knew he felt as bad as I did. After what seemed like ages, he finally replied, "But I can't wait to hold you and kiss you."

'Soon baby, I promise," I responded. When he didn't respond for a while, I added, "Tomorrow night for sure."

I received a text as I was typing this one out saying, "Baby, I need to see you real bad."

I smiled as I could read his eagerness in his words. I loved that he missed me so much because I missed him just as much too, or more if that was possible. So much for out of sight out of mind, I thought to myself grinning.

He texted again with seven kisses and an, "I love you baby".

"I love you too."

"You're all mine; don't forget that." He must be crazy to think I would want anyone else but him.

"Yes, baby. I am all yours."

Somewhere between all our messages, I realised it was time for me to get out of bed and get ready for work. In reality, I did not want to go to work today. It sucked that I had to wait a whole day more to see him. On the other hand, everything seemed to finally be in place. When he was around, it was like everything was better and everything was going to be okay.

But he got busy in his office for being away for a week that I actually could meet him only on his birthday eve. I was pretty excited. It was a Saturday night, perfect time to bring in anyone's birthday. More importantly he would finally see the gift I had gotten made with much love. I went out and bought wrapping paper and carefully wrapped it.

I had only about three hours to get ready. I wanted to wear something just for him. Something he had never seen me in before. I knew just the place where I'd find it, Alisha's closet.

The moment I entered her room, she walked towards the cupboard, opened it and said, "Take what you want."

"How did you know?"

"Doesn't take a genius, you know" she said with one eye brow raised.

"I'm looking for something he would really like. Something that will make him, fall in love with me all over again and yes it has to be kind of sexy."

"I know just the thing, but you have to be careful with it," she said and started laughing.

"How am I supposed to wear this?" I looked at it from all angles trying to figure it out but was quiet lost.

She just couldn't stop laughing at me trying to figure it out and struggling with getting it on me. Finally, when she was done laughing at me she showed me how to wear it. I tried to slide it on and got lost in it despite the demo.

"Help," I yelled out.

She laughed again as she tried to tug and pull and put it in place.

"It's quite hot. I like it. But I hope he does."

"Why wouldn't he? He is a guy; any guy would love it."

"True. But I need something to wear over it for now."

She gave me a white shrug to wear over it and I was finally ready.

When I reached there, I put the collage and the frame in his car and we went to the restaurant. I really wanted him to open it right there but I knew he'd end up opening it only when he was home. So I'd just have to wait.

The evening was pleasant, and when it was nearing midnight, I wanted to be the first one to wish him. But his cousin was there, and I just backed off and decided to wish him after her. I don't know why, but family usually comes first. After cutting the cake and other birthday rituals, we all went out.

There was one thing I noticed though. He kept fidgeting with my clothes, trying to adjust it from here and there, which was unlike him. He was not usually this protective about me.

The only time I had felt it before this was when we I had gone out with Karan, Rohan and some of their friends. Karan's friends were all chatty with me and were asking me to request the DJ to play a particular song of their choice. They were sure he'd listen to my request and play it because it was a pretty girl's request. We were laughing over it, when Rohan had just walked up to me, taken me by my arm and had said, "Find someone else to do this; she is with me." I was surprised when he had done that but his "she is with me" had made me very happy.

But this time, it was different. When we were at the club and dancing close, I noticed he was still trying to adjust my clothes. I began to feel bad and uncomfortable about it. I finally decided to ask him, "Do you not like what I'm wearing?"

"I do baby but you didn't have to like dress up for me."

"I thought you'd like my dressing up for you," I said feeling a bit hurt because I went through all that trouble.

"I like it, immensely; but the problem is that everyone else here also does."

"What you trying to say?"

"I'm saying you don't have to do this for me I love you anyway. Even when you dress how you normally dress. This is not you and I don't want you to change for me in anyway. I love you the way you are."

I smiled.

"Who did you borrow it from?"

"Alisha. How come you're so sure it's not mine?"

"I know you," he said confidently.

I had no idea what to say to that. I still didn't understand why he was just being possessive. He held me closer than he used to and he kept asking me if I was his. I have to confess that after a while, it began to worry me.

He dropped me home at six in the morning next day. I kissed him before getting out of the car and reminded him about the birthday present.

Once I opened the door, I went straight to bed, totally exhausted.

YOURS

I woke up and noticed I had a couple of messages from Rohan saying, "I really like the present baby. You must have spent a lot of time on it. Mom also saw it and liked it."

My heart skipped a beat when I read that his mom liked it. I quickly messaged him again, "Does your mom know who gave it to you?"

"Yes, idiot. I told her it was you. Is that a problem?"

That made me so uneasy. There was something about parents that scared me a little. Especially if it was the parents of the boy I loved so very much.

"No, it's not. Just freaks me out a little."

"Don't think so much, idiot."

Later that day he messaged me, "You sure won't break up with me?"

I was a little surprised when I read that. It was very unlike him to be so insecure and possessive. I didn't have a problem with it, because at this point I loved him so much that I'd do anything for him.

I replied back saying, "Yes, I'm sure I won't."

Just as I had sent that, my friend Kartik called me.

"Hello."

"Hey, what's up?"

"Nothing much. Are we meeting today?"

"Yes, of course. Will see around 8?"

"Yes."

"Gayatri is also coming with a friend of hers." He chuckled at that, I wondered why. He quickly added, "More the merrier"

"What's the plan?" I asked him, to be sure of the time it'd take.

"Was thinking we'll go out drinking and then I could drop you home."

"I was actually thinking I'd catch up with Rohan once we are done."

"That's cool too, either way I'm good. You are really into him, aren't you?" I sensed his smile and replied shyly,

"Yes. Karan, do you remember, in high school, just before we met, I was with this guy and…"

"I definitely remember that. You were totally in love with that dude." he said completing my sentence.

"Well this is the first time after that I have felt this way." I smiled to myself.

"That's a good thing, and I'm so damn happy for you. I hope I get to meet him Soon."

"I could introduce you tonight."

"Sounds good, see you tonight…"

"See you."

I messaged Rohan after this and told him my plan and really hoped he would be free to meet me after that since he said he wouldn't be free to join us before that. He said he would. I was looking forward to the night. I messaged Rohan again a little later.

"I love you baby. Can't wait to see you."

"I love you too baby <3"

"Can I keep it?" I replied referring to the heart he had sent me.

"It's yours baby."

"Just so you know I'm not giving it back. You can keep mine instead."

"You're mine, more than I ever imagined."

I loved it when he said such things and I thought of teasing him a bit, "I have a question."

"When don't you?"

"Shut up, idiot. What does your heart say about me?"

"What kind of question is that?"

"Stop counter questioning, just answer."

"That I should keep you close. I can't afford to lose someone who cares and loves me so much. Being with you is pretty much being in a fairy tale. My heart is yours. I don't have it anymore. Puneet made me realise it today."

"How is that?"

"He made me realise I was in love."

My heart just stopped when I read that. We were in love with each other. It wasn't just me who felt that way. It's not easy finding someone who returns your love and I had.

"I'm in love with you too, like crazy. Don't leave me."

"I won't, idiot. I got to get back to work now. I will see you tonight."

"Can't wait."

CALL MY NAME AND I'LL BE THERE

The four of us started the evening early. I met Gayatri around 6:00 pm. I went to her house we spent time catching up while waiting for her friend and Kartik to join us. It was about an hour later both of them joined us that we decided to head out.

The night started out really well. I had about five shots of Souza Gold tequila, my favourite, and I felt fantastic except one small thing, I was missing Rohan. I usually didn't drink much or even at all when he was not around. This time I knew I was meeting him later, but it was still not the same.

After about two hours of drinking and eating and a continuous flow of crazy conversation, we decided to leave and figure out what to do next.

"I can't believe you had so much to drink and you're still normal." Kartik said as we walked to toward the exit.

"I know, but this tequila is good. I love it."

"I can see that," he said laughing.

"So what's the plan now?" Gayatri asked.

"I don't know. What do you guys want to do?"

"I have some friends meeting up at Khan Market I was thinking we could all join them," Gayatri offered.

"Sounds fine. Anyway, I have to drop her off to her lover boy," Kartik said looking at me with a smirk of his face, nudging me as we walked towards the car.

"You won't stop teasing me about it, will you?" I asked.

He laughed, "I'm happy for you, you seem really happy with this guy. And I know you for a long time now, so I know how much this means to you. It's fun pulling your leg about it a little."

I stayed silent because I didn't know what to say to that. I was happy about it, and Rohan meant a whole lot to me.

"Stop blushing so much," he said as he opened the car door for me.

"I'm trying not to, but you're embarrassing me," I said as I continued to blush.

He just laughed and once we were all in the car, we headed towards our destination.

I messaged Rohan and told him I was going to be there, to which he said that he would join us when he was done with work.

Once we got there, I was actually happy and perfectly set for the evening. We chose the biggest table available and sat down. Now we were about seven people; everyone was ordering their drinks when I was trying to decide what to have. I didn't really want any more alcohol but I figured one more drink would not really harm me.

"They don't have the tequila I like," I said sadly.

"Have something else," Gayatri said followed with a, "Do you want a glass of wine or something?"

"Not in the mood for wine. Besides, I would never mix wine with anything, it never agrees with me."

I studied the menu some more and then I decided to try the tequila with a fancy name that I could not pronounce.

Within fifteen minutes, all our drinks were served. Kartik decided to have a shot with me.

"To you being happy," he said.

"To me being happy."

"Cheers."

I downed the tequila shot in one go. After a few moments, I was feeling so very fucked. I went straight to the loo and started throwing up. Gayatri came to check on me. We went back to the table when I felt better.

"Are you okay?" Kartik asked as I reached the table.

"Yes, I am feeling better. It was really bad quality tequila it's reacting really badly with me."

"I know, I didn't finish my shot." He said feeling a little bad for me.

After a few minutes, again I felt sick again. This time Kartik escorted me. It was very embarrassing. This usually didn't happen and none of my friends had ever seen me like this before. I was sure the tequila was bad and thus all the trouble.

"Hey, are you feeling better?" Kartik asked as I got up and walked out and washed my face.

"I think ..." before I could finish the sentence I was back throwing up.

Kartik came in and held my hair back for me. "Could you call Rohan please," I asked him and passed him my phone. I thought his presence would make me feel better and really wished and wanted him there right now to take care of me.

I don't quite remember much of what happened next. I wasn't drunk at all I was just so completely sick. I remember Gayatri being there and finally, Rohan coming in and helping me. I felt so much more comfortable having Rohan around.

Then I think Kartik walked me down the stairs towards Rohan's car. I could hear some discussion happening as to who was going to drop me home. Obviously Rohan would. He had to. He was mine. After you're in a relationship with someone for so long you just know you can count of them to take care of you and they will.

When we finally reached the car, I knew there was no way I would be able to open the door in my messed up state. I could barely hold myself together, let alone my house keys. I hated this feeling. I called Alisha asking her if she was home. Unfortunately, she was not. I was not really sure how I was going to manage unlocking my door without her around. Rohan told me to stop worrying and that he would take care of me and make sure I was fine.

Through the journey home I had my head comfortably in Rohan's lap. He got me home as soon as he could and carefully helped me all the way to the door. He somehow managed me and managed to open the door as well. And then he actually carried me all the way to my room, helped me get into bed without any difficulty. He even helped change into my night clothes and tucked me into bed like I was a little girl. He made sure I was comfortable before he sweetly kissed me on my forehead, wished me goodnight and left.

And at that moment, I fell in love with him, all over again.

THE NIGHT THAT WAS

The next morning, I woke up without a hangover, but feeling very dazed accompanied with a bad stomach infection. I had a number of messages: one from Gayatri asking me if I was okay and asking me to call her; one from Kartik again checking on me; and then a number of them from Rohan.

Before responding to anyone, I called Rohan. He didn't answer his phone so I went in for a shower to get all clean again. Well, scrub myself is more like it, considering the night before I was practically making love to the bathroom floor.

When I got out, I tried calling Rohan again but he still didn't answer. I then decided to call Gayatri to ask her exactly what happened since I only had a vauge recollection of last night's events.

"Hey, how're you feeling?" she asked as soon as she answered.

"Not that bad actually, I don't have a hangover. Just feeling extremely dazed and I have this bad stomach infection, that's all."

"Well, that's not too bad. The infection explains you're throwing up. You were really sick. I'm guessing you reached home safe."

"I was with Rohan. I'm always safe with him. He was actually incredibly sweet and behaved very unexpectedly. He helped me change and tucked me into bed and just kissed me goodnight, made sure I was okay and then left. I didn't exactly expect him to tuck me in and everything it was incredibly sweet."

"Really... I know that is so sweet."

"I know. I can't believe it. So, anyway, what the hell happened last night? I do remember till I was throwing up and first you were there, then Kartik was there, and Rohan came and helped. But what exactly happened after that, my memory is just a little hazy; you'll have to remind me."

She laughed, "Well, we were all trying to figure out how to get you down the stairs. I thought Rohan would carry you or something but Kartik actually helped you down the stairs. And then Kartik was saying he could drop you back, but Rohan insisted that he would. Kartik backed off then, because Rohan is your boyfriend. And he didn't want to cause any trouble between you two. Then once you were in the car, we guys left."

"Okay," I said, not knowing what else to say.

I said the customary goodbyes and hung up.

Since Rohan had not been answering the calls, I decided to call up Kartik. He didn't answer too, but called back a minute or so later.

"Hey," I said.

"Hi. How are you feeling?"

"Better."

"Hangover..?"

"Nope, just a little dazed," I said laughing.

"Well at least you don't have a hangover."

"Thanks, though, for looking after me. Gayatri told me you helped me down the stairs last night."

"You're welcome. I would do it for anyone. I was even thinking that if you could not go home in that state, then I could have taken you home. That would have led to a lot of explanations to my mom in the morning, but still." He said laughing.

"That would have been really funny."

"I think Rohan doesn't like me." Kartik's tone changed all of a sudden and he sounded serious.

"Why?" I asked, not understanding what he meant to say.

"He didn't seem to like it when I was helping you. I offered to drop you home and he insisted that he'll do it. I didn't want to cause any problems between you and him so didn't say anything. Besides he's your boyfriend, so..."

"I'm sure it's all good and…" I noticed my phone beeping in between; Rohan was calling me back.

"Hey listen, Rohan is calling me…"

Before I finished the sentence, he said, "Okay, sure, you talk to him. Bye."

By the time he hung up, Rohan had already cut the call. I don't know why he never let it ring and wait for me to answer. He should know I would always answer his call. I threw these thoughts off and called him back.

"Hello," he said in a blank tone.

"Hey, thanks for last night baby and I am so sorry I didn't get to spend time with you. I really wanted to." I felt so bad and guilty about it.

"It's okay, don't worry about it," he said sounding standoffish.

"Will make up for it the next time I see you. Promise."

"Okay."

"Can you meet today?" I asked him.

"I don't know, let's see. Anyway I got to go now. I have work to do, so will call you later."

"Okay. I love you, bye."

"Love you too. Bye."

For a moment, I was a little worried because he sounded so distant and it felt like he was pushing me away but when he said he loved me too, I felt better.

He didn't call me back for the rest of the day. I kept waiting, thinking he would. Then finally, I called him before I was going to sleep. He again said he was busy and didn't have time to talk, but he would see me tomorrow evening. I just said goodnight and hung up, feeling really bad.

I decided to SMS him since he was too busy to talk. I sent him a message immediately, "Baby, why are you pushing me away? I'm sorry. I didn't mean to get that sick last night. I did want to spend time with you and I was really looking forward to it. I just ended having some really bad tequila and that's why I fell sick. I said I would make it up to you. And I am glad that you came and took care of me. I love you even more for that."

Shortly after he responded saying, "It's not about that and I will always be there when you need me."

"Okay, I love you."

"Love you too."

I felt a little better after getting that off my chest and I felt safe again, knowing he would always be there. I decided to just go to sleep and not worry about it anymore.

I woke about an hour later after a having a really bad dream that I could not remember. But it left me feeling weird and I couldn't get any sleep after that. I called Rohan up again.

"Hello."

"Hey! How's the day going? I had a really bad dream," I said sadly.

"Why baby?"

"I don't know. I wish you were here with your arms around me. I miss you so much."

"I wish that too, baby."

"Can't wait to see you tomorrow."

"Me Too."

I smiled, "Okay. I'm feeling better; going back to sleep now. Goodnight."

"Goodnight baby, sleep well and have sweet dreams this time."

"You too, whenever you sleep."

"Love you, idiot."

"Love you too," I said laughing.

"Bye."

"Bye."

BIRTHDAY PLANS

It was a month later and it was almost time for my birthday. I met him one evening. He picked me up and we went to Defence Colony to have a few drinks and just spend time together.

As we walked up the stairs to our usual place, he spanked me. I turned around and held his hand while I climbed the rest of the stairs. He knew he was being naughty and flashed me his cute little boy irresistible smile. He really was totally and absolutely adorable.

We walked towards the corner table where we pretty much usually sat. It was very cold, the air conditioner was in full blast and the vents were facing us directly. We asked the waiter to turn it down, but it didn't make too much difference. So I simply snuggled up close to him. I guess it worked out for the best.

"Very smart," he said as I slowly found my way into his arms to keep myself warm.

"It is cold in here and you're supposed to keep me warm. It's your job."

"Uh huh, my job it seems."

"Yes, one of your many duties as my boyfriend," I said with a big smile plastered on my face.

"Idiot," he said as he put his arm around me.

He then ordered his usual and a tequila sunrise for me. While we waited for our drinks, we talked about my birthday plans.

"So, what do you want for your birthday?"

At first I didn't want to tell him what I wanted and just wanted to know what he would come up with on his own.

"I don't know. You just get me whatever you want to."

"Why can't you just tell me?"

He sounded so pained, I felt a little sorry. Besides I did want something, so I decided I would just be nice and tell him.

"Okay, since it's my 25th birthday, I want something in silver. Because 25th birthday is always silver. There is this thing I like. It's a silver bracelet and it has a red heart on it. And also I want a charm, it's an angel wing. The idea is that I will always have your heart with me and the angel wing is for protection. Did you understand, like you're always there for or with me type of thing." I tried so hard not to blush as I said that.

"Your such a little idiot, you need a bracelet to know you have my hear or that I will always be there for you."

I looked a little worried and before I could say anything he quickly added.

"Sure baby, whatever you want."

I heard him say these words and wondered to myself how I got so lucky to find such an amazing guy. He didn't even think twice. I was a little speechless when he said that, so I just kissed him gently on the cheek and pulled away quickly as the waiter approached and placed our drinks on the table. I was a little embarrassed as I pulled away, but as usual, he put me at ease as he kissed me gently on my forehead.

"So what do you want to do?"

"Now...?" I asked a little confused.

"Not now, I meant on your birthday."

"Well I want to just spend it with you mostly. My family usually flies down but this year they aren't so just you and me and maybe over the weekend later could do something with my friends."

"I like you and me. What do you have in mind?"

"Well, I was thinking we could if you're okay with it, get out of the city and stay together for a couple of days, a romantic weekend getaway." I was nervous for I wasn't sure what he'd think of the idea. Even thought we had gotten really serious we hadn't yet really talked about taking trips together.

"We could work it out," he said with a smile.

"You sure you wouldn't mind that?"

"Don't ask me stupid questions. Why would I mind spending time with you, idiot?"

"Just checking," I said. I was so happy. This would be so perfect.

"Why're you being so nice to me?"

He laughed, "Again," he said followed with a, "You want me to be mean to you?"

"No. I like you being nice."

"Then what's your problem?"

"Just not used to it, someone being this nice. We have been together so long and usually by this time things change a lot."

He just smiled and said, "Then get used to it."

"I am, slowly. Just don't make me have to get unused to it later."

"Uh huh, you think too much. I told you I'm not going anywhere."

"Okay, you better not be."

"Idiot," he whispered into my ear.

I smiled.

I was looking forward to the ten days to my birthday, which would culminate in my first ever holiday with the love of my life.

HAPPY BIRTHDAY TO ME

Ten days passed by in a blink and it was finally the eve of my birthday.

It had been a very exhausting day. I stayed back at work till late and then came home and worked some more. But I didn't care much about it because in a few hours, I was going to be 25, and would celebrate it with the guy I was so deeply in love with. I had half a mind to just switch my phone off and go to sleep because I was so tired. But I knew I couldn't I couldn't miss Rohan calling me. So I just got into bed, turned the lights off and tried to get a little sleep, knowing I will be woken up soon enough.

Before the clock struck 12, my phone went beeping in quick succession with messages and phone calls. But my personal favourite wish was the one where Rohan called saying he'd see me in an hour to kiss me happy birthday – a wonderful beginning to my special birthday.

As promised, one hour later he was there at my doorstep. The moment I opened my door, he just held me in his arms and kissed me. I smiled as I saw him, brimming with love for me. He picked me up, put me on the table, kissed me a little more and then without any words, he took my hand and put the bracelet on my wrist. It was perfect, exactly the way I had wanted it.

"Happy birthday baby," he whispered into my ear and before I could say anything, he kissed me again and hugged me tight.

He let go when my sister walked into the room, turned on the light and in a very annoyed voice said, "Some people have work tomorrow."

We both laughed.

"You got your chance to wish her; it's my turn now," Rohan

said as he ignored my sister.

"You guys are hopeless," she yelled and switched the light off and went back to bed.

"Room?" he said with that cute boy look in his eyes.

I laughed, "Baby, howsoever much I would love the 'room' idea, I have to go to work tomorrow and should get my sleep for that."

"So no room," he said with a sad face.

Sometimes he really was like a little baby boy I needed to take care of. I kissed him a few times more before I said, "Baby, in just a few hours we will meet again and we will be together for two whole days."

He looked at me with a straight face and said, "I guess."

"I can't wait. I really wish we could leave right now."

"Let's go," he said.

"Are you crazy?" I said, secretly really liking that option.

"I want you time."

"I want you time too, but work tomorrow," I said as I got off the table. We reached the front door and finally kissed goodbye.

"Happy birthday once again baby, will see you soon."

"You better. I love you," I said as I pulled him back, and kissed him one last time.

"I love you, too," he said as he kissed me on my forehead.

"Okay, go now, idiot," I said biting my lip slightly, controlling the wide grin that had come to play on my lips.

He left me there, standing at the door, feeling just watching as he walked down the driveway and out of sight.

ROMANTIC GETAWAY

This was going to be the best birthday ever, and I just knew it. I was supposed to meet him at night and have a romantic dinner and then we were to stay together for the next two nights. It was going to be our first ever trip together.

The loud ring of my phone startled me and brought me back to reality. It was my mom calling to wish me. I loved spending my birthday with my family. Sometimes they would fly down and surprise me but this year my birthday was bang in the middle of the week. After my long conversation with my parents, I sadly headed off to work. When it was finally night time, I was sitting alone, wondering what was taking him so long. I called him a few times. He said he was really busy with work and he would get out soon.

Minutes left like hours. It was almost ten and he was still busy with no sign of leaving. I began to get really upset. I was really looking forward to this trip. I tried to understand that he had work and it was important, but birthdays come just once in a year and this one was really important to me.

In my very irritable mood, I messaged him saying, "By the time you actually see me, my birthday will be over."

He replied saying he was sorry and he'd come as soon as he could.

He finally did arrive at 11:45 pm, fifteen minutes before my anger touched zenith.

I was happy when I saw the headlights of his car brighten the otherwise really dark road. I got into the car and for some reason in that one brief moment; I forgot about all my irritation as he leant in and kissed me. I guess at the end of it all, I was happy he was there, and the days ahead held more happiness than these few hours of waiting.

It was a long drive and I was a bit tired, so I lay my head on his shoulder and slept. I loved doing that because every time there was a red signal and he stopped the car, he would have his arm on me to make sure I was okay and it felt nice and safe.

Once we reached the resort my excitement tripled. Rohan could feel my impatience as he was taking care of the check-in process and gently held my hand as we approached our room.

He then suggested we go down to the bar and have a drink or too. I decided to change and wear a nice dress for the occasion. Once we reached the bar. He ordered a bottle of pink champagne for the two of us.

I didn't drink much maybe just about half a glass initially when the waiters brought out a small cake.

Rohan looked at me and smiled as I cut the cake and fed him a bite.

"I wanted it to be special," he whispered into my ear.

"Thank you."

"There is one more thing." He said as he gave a bouquet of flowers.

"Twenty five red roses and one white one for luck." He explained with a grin on his face.

I smiled, "idiot."

After the drinks and cake we decided to go back to our room and order room service as both of us were beginning to feel hungry. We had ordered way more than we knew we could eat. While waiting for dinner, we got into bed and watched some TV.

He pulled me close and wrapped his arms around me as I lay back comfortably against him.

"We are finally here," he said.

I looked into his eyes and said, "Thank you". I took his hand in mine, fingers intertwined and let his love warm me.

He took my hand to his lips and kissed it softly. "Happy birthday baby," he said again.

"I love being home," he said as he put his arm around me and kissed me gently on my forehead.

I wished I could just freeze this moment in time and go back to it whenever I wanted.

A little while later, the bell rang and both of us looked at each other wondering who was going to open the door.

"Please," he said looking at me.

"No way, you go. My birthday; my rules," I said, sounding like a spoiled little princess.

He laughed. The bell rang again.

"Go," I said pushing him off the bed.

He gave me a half grumpy, half smile look as he walked towards the door.

Once we had the room to ourselves again, I asked him if I could borrow something to wear. He gave me one of his t shirts. I loved wearing his clothes because they reminded me of him and made me feel close to him when he was not around. I slipped into it and joined him at the table for dinner. By this time we were both so hungry we polished off the food in no time. It was good we ordered extra.

When we got back into bed, I lay back into his arms and fell asleep almost instantly.

The next morning or rather afternoon, I woke up before he did. I brushed my teeth and went back into bed, not knowing exactly what else to do. I was wondering if I should wake him up or let him sleep. He looked so peaceful in his sleep that I didn't feel like disturbing him. So I waited. When he showed no signs of waking up for the next half an hour, I tried to wake him up.

I slid right beside him till there was space left between us. I first gently kissed him on his cheek, at which he didn't even budge. I then ran my fingers up and down his chest, hoping it would tickle him a little, but seeing no effect, I started to get a little naughty. He was sleeping like a log, not reacting to anything I did, and just when I was about to give up, he grabbed me and started tickling me till I couldn't control my giggles. He then pulled me close, hugged me and went back to sleep, and this time I joined him.

By the time we both finally woke up, it was about 2:00 pm. We got the room cleaned while we showered and got ready. After that, we were both back in bed trying to figure out what to do.

"Do you want to watch a movie? I have some on my laptop."

"I wouldn't mind. We could ask them if they have any DVDs. Usually they do keep some," I suggested.

"Sounds okay to me. Why don't you call and find out?"

I laughed because I knew he would say that. I called them and they sent up a list of movies to the room. We spent half an hour trying to find a movie we both didn't mind watching and finally settled for *Wall Street*.

I lay back in his arms as we watched the movie. Once the movie was over we wondered again what to do. This time we watched *Cars* on his laptop and we ordered dinner to accompany the movie.

The moment the movie was over, even before the credits started rolling, he moved the laptop away, pulled me closer and started kissing me.

"Baby, can I get a massage please," I asked attempting to persuade him with my puppy dog face. I realised I really didn't need that, because he agreed immediately.

I have to admit: getting a massage from your boyfriend is way better than one from a stranger at a massage parlour. It was sweet and romantic.

His stokes were soft and firm, he was better than I thought he'd be. Every time he even tried to get near my feet, I started giggling. Soon enough I forgot all about the giggling and got lost in the relaxing pleasure of his massage.

After an hour he was finally done and I found that pampering session perfect addition to our romantic getaway.

"I really loved it," I said.

"I'm glad you did."

"I did. I have never gotten a massage like this before."

"Ever?" he asked staring at me in complete disbelief.

"Never ever before," I said and kissed him.

He put his arm around me and hugged me tight.

"I'm glad I'm the first one."

"You're the first for many things baby, I just guess I kind of saved all the sweet romantic things till I found someone I really cared about and who was extremely special to me to share it with and here you are." I said smiling.

With a big grin on his face he said, "I'm glad."

"So this is you making up for meeting me late?" I asked.

He smiled, "I would have done it either way."

"Could I interest you in a hot bath with me?" I asked.

"I'm not in the mood for the tub. It's 3:00am."

"So…"

"You're crazy."

"It will be fun."

"I'm sure it will be, but I really don't feel like it."

"Okay," I said feeling a little disappointed. "I will go alone then. If you change your mind, you can always join me."

"Uh-huh."

I got off the bed and got a hot bath ready for myself. Once it was hot enough, I got into the tub and lay there feeling completely relaxed and totally enjoying the moment. Not more than three minutes later, Rohan walked in holding two glasses of champagne.

I laughed, "I thought you were not in the mood."

"Naked you in the tub, how could I not join!" His eyes sparkled with naughtiness.

I laughed, "Idiot."

"So is this also a first time thing?" he asked.

I blushed, "yes."

He smiled as he moved a little closer and kissed me. We stayed there in the tub talking, laughing and drinking champagne. It was nice. I had never done something like this before. It was always something I would watch on TV or see in a movie and I would wonder if I would ever find someone I'd want to do that with.

About twenty minutes later, we got out of the tub, had a shower and went to bed. I was not too keen to go sleep because I knew when we woke up in the morning, this would all be over and it would be time for the mundane stuff again.

CONFUSED

The next morning, we left for home and as he dropped me, something strange happened. He got a call from one of his friends and he lied about where he was last night. I was not sure why he would lie to his friends about being with me. I had met all his friends and they all knew about me. I could not help but wonder if he didn't want them to know we were taking holidays together.

"Why did you lie to him?"

"What do you mean?" He sounded taken back at the question.

"Why didn't you tell them you were with me?"

"How does it matter?"

"It feels like you don't want them to know we are together." I said, not knowing exactly what sense to make of it.

"It's not like that they know we are together. How does that even matter? As long as I know and you know, why do you need the whole world to know?"

"I'm not saying tell the whole world. It just feels like you don't want this."

"I'm here with you, am I not?"

"Are you happy being with me?"

"I am happy with you. I just don't like the whole relationship thing and you know that."

I didn't know what to say to that. It's not like I planned this to take this course; it just happened. When we go into it, we never wanted the whole serious relationship thing. But somewhere along the way, things changed. We fell in love. I thought he was happy with the way things had turned out.

"Now you're going to be quiet?" he said sounding annoyed.

"I just don't know what to say to that. You just completely out of the blue say something like that to me, how am I supposed to react?"

"I'm not saying I don't want to be with you or that I don't love you. I do love you okay."

"Okay, I love you too." I said looking him right in the eye. In some way I was trying to see if I still saw what I did the first time I looked into his eyes.

I felt a little uncomfortable about what he had said. I understood what he meant about the whole serious relationship thing, but I had thought now we were in it he wanted this as much as I did.

DISTANCE

I met him a few days later and found him busy in a meeting. I sat with his friends and waited. I knew we had crazy work hours, and waiting was inevitable if we had to make most of our time.

I mostly felt a little bored with his friends; not that I didn't like them or anything, just that Rohan had become extremely possessive of me, so I never really tried to get to know them. It didn't really matter to me anyway.

I sat there in silence for a while, waiting for him to get done with the meeting. It was then that his friend started talking to me all of a sudden about general stuff like where I stayed, what I did, etc., and so I responded and talked for a while. Then again there was silence again.

I messaged Rohan, "How long do you think you'd take? I'm getting really bored."

He responded saying, "About five or ten minutes. And can you stop flirting with my friends?"

I was a little taken aback by that comment. What was wrong with him? Didn't he know I was his? I was merely responding out of courtesy. I really did not understand what had gotten into him lately he had been acting different.

"I'm not flirting. He was just talking to me generally."

"I hope so."

"You are mad. I'm yours."

"You better be :*"

"Well I am and I miss you. So hurry up."

I was not used to him being so insecure or possessive. I didn't understand why he would even think I would ever flirt with his friend. This made me so conscious that when I was out with him and his friends, I'd keep quiet for most of the time because I didn't want him to think I was flirting with any of them and it sucked because I would just be even more bored than before. Plus, I couldn't really talk to him also because it would be awkward to have a private conversation with him when there were so many people around. I could notice his attention dwindling towards me. Initially he used to check on me and make sure I was comfortable. But lately, I would just be standing there and feeling extremely bored. He just pretended that he didn't realize I was getting bored, and at times it seemed he had forgotten I was there with him.

This whole thing went on for a month or two and now every time on a Saturday night when he used to go out with his friends and he called me, even if I knew I could go, I would usually just say no because I knew I would end up getting get bored. From there on, it got worse.

One evening I was with him, and Karan was also there. I was craving to spend some quality time with Rohan because we hadn't been spending as much time together like we used to, but couldn't. So I didn't say much and was getting a little bored as usual when Laksh called me up.

"Hello."

"Hey, where are you?" He sounded chirpy.

"I'm out with Rohan and Karan at Toro, Khan Market. It's an awesome place amazing Sangria and delicious food. Why don't you join us? I'm a little bored anyway. They're both talking and I'm like a little left out types."

"Okay! I'll be there in about twenty minutes."

"Awesome."

"Bye."

"Bye."

When Laksh reached there, he had got a friend of his along and we all sat and talked. Since I was finally talking, I was happy and not bored anymore. However, I didn't realize that this would make things between me and Rohan worse.

YOU'RE EVERYTHING TO ME

I don't know if separation is in the air today
But you just seem so far away
The distance in your voice cuts like a knife
I'm here
I'm yours
All I want is for you to hold me
Wish you were here
Wish you were close
I need to feel safe again
It's always you
It's only you
No one else can make me feel the way you do
You're all I know
You're all I want
Stay with me
Stay close
Nothing means anything without you
Baby you're everything to me
You're everything I need
So please don't let me go
I know you've been in love before
And I know it's let you down
But my hearts in your heart
If I break yours
Then I break mine
I'm too much into this
I've fallen too deep
I don't know what tomorrow brings
And I want to find out
With you by my side
'Coz you're everything to me.

FOR BETTER OR FOR WORSE

I called him up the next day, and told him we needed to talk because things were not the same and I didn't understand what was happening to us.

"So talk." He said in a very garish tone.

I didn't like the way he said that, like it didn't matter to him at all and I was just making a deal about nothing.

"What's gotten into you?"

"Nothing's gotten into me; what's gotten into you?" He said raising his voice a little.

"Why are you being rude?"

"What do you think am I doing?"

It felt as if I was speaking to someone I didn't know at all. I didn't even know what to say to say to him. He was not usually like this.

"I don't know, you're just pushing me away."

"How am I pushing you away?"

"The way you're behaving."

"Everything is *my* fault, isn't it? I'm being rude. I'm pushing you away. You never have anything to do with it."

I was beginning to feel confused. "What's going on in your mind? Can you please just talk to me and tell me. What's on your mind?"

"Nothing is on my mind, okay. I don't have anything to say to you."

"I know you, okay. Can you not lie to me?"

"What do you want from me?"

"I just want to talk. That's all."

"Really?"

"What's that supposed to mean?"

"Well you seem to be more interested in talking to your friends than to me."

"What are you talking about? I came all the way to meet you."

"Yes, but then you don't say anything. You don't talk to me anymore, you're all weird and quiet and when your friends come, then somehow you have so much to talk about."

"It's not like that, Rohan."

"Really, then please explain to me what it's like."

"When I come there, I come to see you. Not your friends. And every time I'm there, your friends are there too. I'm not saying it's a problem; but I need time with you too."

"But you don't talk to me also; it's not like I'm not there."

"How will I be comfortable when your friends are taking so much of your attention and you're busy with them?"

"What do you want me to do? Ask them to leave because you can't speak to me in their presence?" he said sounding extremely irritated.

"That's not what I'm saying to you. All I am saying is that I get bored and when I talk to them, you accuse me of flirting and then when I don't say anything, then this…"

"So, I'm not asking you to talk to them, you can talk to me."

I didn't know how to explain to him that it was a little difficult to focus on and speak only to him when we were all out together in a big group. The worst part was that even if I wanted to talk to him, by the time we did get time with each other, I was either too tired or just too irritated. I'd end up kissing him goodnight and pretending all was well, when the reality of the situation was that I missed him like crazy and was desperately waiting to spend some quality time with him. I just wanted my boyfriend back - the one who loved spending time with me. The truth was I missed him. I missed being friends with him like we were. Before anything else we were friends and we had become the best of friends but somehow it was like the relationship had gotten in the way of our friendship.

"All that is fine, Rohan, but I need time with you. I love you and when I come to meet you, I really look forward to spending time with just *you*. And that never seems to work out because your friends are there, throughout."

He didn't say anything for a while. I waited for him to say something, but he still didn't.

"Say something," I implored.

"It's not like I don't want to spend time with you. We will figure it out, okay."

"Okay and I will do better with the talking. I love you."

That's the boy I knew and loved, who no matter what happened or how bad it was, would always find some way to figure it out.

"I love you too."

In the one year I had known him no matter what happened between us, whether it was a disagreement or a misunderstanding the one thing we had was communication. We always talked to each other about how we felt and every single time we had any problem we always figured it out and made it work.

I know I believe in fairytales but in real life we build our own fairytales. Nobody really knows what happens after the princess and prince fall in love. We are just told to believe that they live happily ever after.

RED WINE

The coming Saturday we went to Shiros with a friend of his. This time he was nice; he was being himself. He paid attention to me like he used to. He made sure I didn't feel left out.

When we went to the bar, he asked me what I wanted to drink.

"Wine, red wine," I said.

He ordered our drinks and then when we got our glasses, we went and joined his friends again. By the time I finished half my glass, I was already feeling light headed. This time he kept me close and held me. I missed being in his arms so much. For the last few months there had been a distance between us which seemed to be reducing now.

"Already?" he asked as I almost tripped while walking.

"It is a really strong wine," I said holding on to him.

He laughed, "It was this time."

It was almost 2:30 am when we left from there. When we reached the car, I sat in my designated place right next to him near the driver's seat. It always irritated me when I was with him and his friends would sit in what I believe was my place.

The night was nice. Well, it was fine till it was 3:00 am. We were at his friend's house and I was beginning to get annoyed because again we had been with his friend almost the entire evening. The moment his friend left the room and I was alone with him, I turned to him and said, "I have to be home soon."

"Okay," he said.

I thought he would understand that I wanted to spend time with him and would leave. But I was wrong. We stayed for another hour or so and then he finally dropped me home. I was upset at the way things were shaping up between the two of us.

When I got home, I walked straight out of the car and into my house. This was perhaps the first time I didn't kiss him when he dropped me and it felt horribly wrong.

Once I had changed into my night clothes and was in bed, I messaged him.

"You've changed."

"I have changed? You are the one who just walked off."

"You could have stopped me. You have done that before."

"I just don't know what you want anymore."

"I just want you. I miss my best friend." I typed out, almost in tears.

He didn't reply. I waited for a while, then finally just gave up and decided to call him and sort this out. I hated it when things were like this between us. It was not supposed to be this way.

"Hello," he answered finally on like the tenth ring.

"Hey, can we talk?"

"Sure, talk!" He said as if he didn't care.

"You didn't reply," I said, not really knowing what to say. It had already begun to feel like a lost cause.

"I don't know what to say."

"Just tell me what's on your mind? Please," I said feeling extremely helpless with this situation.

"What do you want me to say ya?"

I hated it when he talked to me like that. Every time he was irritated or wanted to piss me off, he would end his sentences in 'ya'. I tried to stay calm and not let it get to me.

"Whatever is on your mind, can you please talk to me about it rather than behaving the way you have been?"

"I'm not thinking anything." He sounded so distant; I thought he was building a castle around his feelings, which I could not enter.

"Don't lie! You've been thinking something for sure. It's just that you're not telling me."

"What's your problem?"

When he said that, it hurt like a knife slicing through my heart. My problem? My problem was that I loved him and I didn't know what to do because at this moment he was not letting me love him; he was just pushing me away.

"I don't have a problem. You keep saying you will find time, etc., but it's always still the same."

"I was with you and you didn't even kiss me when I dropped you home. You just walked off."

"Did you even for once wonder why I just walked off?"

He didn't say a thing.

I continued, "I was pissed off. I wanted to spend time with you but you wanted to spend the one hour I could have alone with you with your friend."

"How was I supposed to know that you wanted to spend time?"

"Really! This is what it has now come to? You don't know if I want to spend time with you?"

"It's not like you said anything."

"I told you I had to be home soon but that didn't seem to make a difference."

"I'm sorry."

"I don't understand why you're treating me like this? What did I ever do to you?"

"You didn't do anything like that. It's not you."

I laughed in my head when he said that, the famous it's not you it's me line, classic!

"Then what is it? Why are you hurting me, again and again?" I asked as I finally broke into tears.

"I don't know. I can't do this."

"What do you mean you can't do this?" I asked as my heart started racing. I felt nervous and scared.

"I can't be with you anymore. I can't keep fighting with you. I don't want to hurt you."

For a moment I didn't say anything. I could barely believe what I had just heard. Finally somehow I finally blurted out, "So you would just rather leave?"

"I'm not leaving you. I'm here. I just can't do this serious relationship thing with you."

"What do you mean? What is it that you want then?" I asked, afraid of what I was going to hear.

"Let's just please be friends," he said. His voice was really low.

When he said that, it felt like someone had just punched me really hard in the stomach. I didn't know if I was imagining this or was it real. My head was spinning and I felt like I was going to choke. I could barely focus; I could barely breathe. How could he have just said that? How could my so called boyfriend just all of a sudden stop loving me?

He said it without even flinching, like it was the easiest thing to do or say. Like I didn't matter to him; like the time we spent together didn't matter. It was like I fell off his mind. Like he forgot about me and all the special moment and memories we shared. In that one moment I felt completely screwed up.

"What?" I asked, not knowing what else to say. I was so shocked that the words barely came out of my mouth.

"Can we be friends for a while and figure it out?"

I could feel my heart break, shatter, bleed.

"How can you say that like that? Like it's the easiest thing to say? Like you don't care anymore?"

"I do care about you. I told you it's not about you. It's about me."

"I really don't know what to say," I said as I started to cry again.

"Stop crying, please."

I couldn't stop.

"Please stop crying. I don't like it when you cry like this. I don't want to hurt you and that's the reason I said we should be friends."

'Friends,' I began to detest that word. Was he really serious? How did he expect me to all of a sudden stop loving him like I did and be just friends? Obviously it seemed easy enough for him to do, since he said it so many times. He claimed he doesn't want to hurt me, but he just did.

"I can't be just friends with you," I said.

"I don't know what else to do," he said sounding helpless.

"How about just be with me."

As far as I was concerned, it was simple. If you love someone, you'd want to be with them. If you don't want to be with them, you don't love them, you never did. It was as simple as that.

"I can't," he said.

I really didn't know what else to say so I stayed silent, listening to the sound of his breath.

After some moments of silence I finally spoke, "I guess there is nothing else to say. Goodnight," I said as I choked on my words.

He didn't respond for a while. I was wondering if I should hang up. Maybe he didn't have anything at all to say to me anymore. I waited and started to cry again. It hurt. I couldn't breathe. I felt claustrophobic, like someone was choking me to death.

"Stop crying please...I love you," he said in a tender voice.

"Stop saying that please," I requested. My voice was muffled by the sound of my crying. "Don't tell me you love me and then tell me you want to leave."

He didn't say a word. I knew he felt bad but how could I believe him when he was so easily willing to let me go.

"I should go to sleep now," I said.

"Okay, but please stop crying."

"I have," I said. My tears had stopped at least for that moment.

"You're going to lie to me now?"

My heart broke as I heard those words. He said it to me in his sweet voice that had always made my heart skip a beat and now those same words stung.

"I wouldn't lie to you," I said. I meant every word of it, from my heart. I wish he knew how much I loved him.

"Goodnight, I will call you tomorrow," he said.

"Goodnight," I said as I disconnected the call.

I closed my eyes and I wished that I would never have to wake up again. I didn't want to be without him. He was my world and it felt like my world was now crashing all around me.

I CAN'T BREATHE
I can't breathe.
I'm broken,
I'm torn.
I have been here before.
Sitting here like this,
on the bathroom floor.
I don't have the strength.
I can't stand up.
I cry… till I can't breathe.
And then I cry some more.
I know it's not worth it.
Shedding so many tears,
for someone who doesn't
Know how to love.
It's funny.
How just one thing,
can make everything else
All seem like a lie.
It's funny.
How the word 'friends',
can make you want to die.

VANISHING LOVE

Sleep evaded me. I couldn't get all this off my mind and it hurt immensely. I messaged him hoping that somewhere in his heart he would feel the love I have for him. Somehow maybe he would come back to his senses and tell me he was being crazy and couldn't live without me.

"What happened to us? You used to love me and now every time you say something to me, there is hatred in your voice... I know u said I irritate u, but nothing I'm doing has changed... The more I look at us fall apart, the more I see how much I stayed the same and how much you have changed... You made me feel so loved and now it's like you have forgotten it all? Now it all just hurts so much... I keep crying but the pain only increases. You say you're sorry but things are still the same. It's like you have now become selfish and mean. You talk to me as if I'm out to hurt you. But you don't see that I'm the one who's hurt, that I'm the one broken. I used to be able to be me around you, was able to tell you everything I felt. You used to be my best friend, my shield, anchor, support; and now you're the one bringing me down and watching me break, bit by bit, like you don't care at all. Why do you have so much negativity towards us or me? What did I do to you? You're still my baby and I still love you. But what will I do with a broken heart?"

I looked at my phone a number of times. He had not replied. I finally just fell asleep in exhaustion.

The next day, I dragged myself to work. I was emotionally and mentally numb and in a complete mess. I knew I had to somehow put myself together and survive the day. I checked my phone several times again; he still hadn't replied. I can explain how I got through half a day in just one simple word, 'torture'.

I sat there with my friends and colleagues, seeing them happy and chatting, like it usually was every day. This time, however, instead of joining in the merriment, I sat back and watched. I hoped to feel something but I was numb. I was empty and lost. I tried to control my tears because I didn't want anyone to know how broken I was. Not yet as I had barely accepted it myself, or even understood it. I knew I had to someday, but the question was how.

CAN YOU READ MY TEARS
There is chatter all around.
But I just stare into space.
I'm lost here.
The world is not the same.
I want to talk to you.
To say something,
Reach out.
But I have no words.
I'm hurt.
There is nothing more I can say.
Can you read my tears?
I miss you.
I feel empty inside.
It's like nothing else matters,
without you by my side.
I don't know how to move on,
or how to let go of the pain.
I feel like hating you.
And sometimes I even do.
But I really can't leave.
I don't know how.
Maybe it's easy for you.
But it's not for me.
Because,
I can't stop loving you ...

ALL WE NEED IS A BIT OF PATIENCE

I left from office as soon I could that day. I could not concentrate on anything. It was almost 7:00 pm when I reached home. I was wondering if I should call him or not. I tried to distract myself by watching some television but couldn't. I just kept switching from one channel to another, sometimes not even bothering to look up at the screen to see what was on.

"Aleah!"

I heard my sister scream my name. Normally something like that would startle me but I just kept staring into space, ignoring her completely. She came up to me, took the remote from my hand and switched the television off.

"We need to talk," she said in a tone that made me look up.

"What do you want?" I grunted, not wanting to be disturbed from my wallowing.

"Will you please just tell me what's happening?"

"I just... I don't want to talk about it right now, please," I said and I started crying again.

"It's okay, you don't have to," she said as she put her arms around me and let me cry. "Don't worry so much, you guys always figure it out, don't you?"

"We didn't just fight this time... he said..." I paused to catch my breath between my crying and speaking, "He said he wanted to be friends."

I was choking and couldn't stop crying. My sister just hugged me tight and let me cry for what was something like an hour and a half. Finally when I could catch my breath, I told her what had happened.

"What did you say?"

"I don't know. I could barely think. I was not sure what to say. We started out as friends and we used to be best of friends but we were together and we got so close to each other I can't just switch feelings like that. I just didn't want him to leave me like this. I told him to just stay with me and that I loved him and that we would figure it out like we always do. I also said that I just didn't understand any of this and why he would want to hurt me. He told me it was him not me and well; we all know what a bullshit line that is. Anyway, I didn't know what to say to that and I told him that I can't be friends with him and that he should not leave me. He was the one who always said he would never give on me so easily and not let me go. Then he said he isn't going anywhere and he still loves me." I stopped to catch my breath.

"I just don't get it. How can he say he loves me but then just leave me like that."

"Do you believe him?"

"What do you mean?"

"Do you believe that he loves you?"

I stopped to think for a while. Then I finally said, "I don't know what to think but in my heart I know this is not right. This is not the way it's supposed to be. I know he loves me. I just don't understand what's going on or maybe I just want to believe he does and I'm just fooling myself. I just don't know anything anymore."

"I know what you mean. Even I don't know what to say. Have you spoken to him since?"

"No, I haven't. I have thought about it. Messaging him or calling but then…" my voice trailed off and after a while I added… "I just don't know what to say to him."

"He has not contacted you either?"

"No." I said feeling overwhelmed again.

"So you're just not going to talk to him now?"

"I don't know."

Neither of us said anything for a while. We both sat there next to each other. I know my sister wanted to help me but what could she have done when I felt so lost in the labyrinth of love.

"You think I should talk to him or something?" I asked her, since he usually always had the right answers.

She smiled, "Well, I think to start with, you should wait for him to call you."

"And then what?" I asked, "What am I supposed to say to him?"

"Let him do the talking."

"But what if he doesn't call?" I asked feeling anxious again.

"If he meant what he said, about him still having feelings for you, then he should call. He will."

"So what am I supposed to do till then? Just wait?"

"No, you're supposed to cheer up. Take some time to wallow if you have to, just some time for yourself. Come on, let's have some ice cream and watch some cheesy movie."

I really wanted to decline the offer because I was in no mood to do any of those things. I just wanted to forget all this; to run away and disappear for a while. But then again, I didn't want my sister to worry too much about me, so I agreed.

I faked a smile as we walked to the kitchen and served ourselves two huge scoops of chocolate chip ice cream each. We then decided to watch *Someone Like You,* a movie I'd have really liked, especially in a break-up situation.

I tried to enjoy the movie, but ended up staring at the television, feeling blank and numb. There were scenes in the movie that made me miss him so much. I really didn't know what to do. Should I try and make it work? Should I give up? Should I believe in us? Fight for him? I couldn't take it anymore.

"Hey, I'm going to bed, feeling really tired," I said, as I got up and started walking towards my room.

"Okay, goodnight. Sleep well," she yelled out.

"You too."

Just before getting into bed, I checked my phone to see if there was any call or message from him. There was nothing.

FEELS LIKE THE END OF THE WORLD TO ME

And it feels like the end of the world to me.
I feel choked.
I can barely breathe.
I cry.
Hoping it would ease the pain.
I know my tears will not
Bring him back to me.
But I can't seem to stop.
I feel empty,
Lost, confused.
I drag my feet to work and back.
Somehow making it through
Yet another day
He is the habit
I don't know how to do without.
I remember now
why I protected my heart
For the last seven years.
But this time
I just couldn't help myself
when he kissed me,
His blood ran through my veins.
Only I know
How much of me is lost in him;
Did love die?
Or dwindle into oblivion?
Maybe it was not strong enough,
Maybe it never was,
Maybe I was just
Fooling myself all along.
But I'm too attached now.
There is nothing I can do
Except sit back
And watch my heart break.

JUST FRIENDS?

The next morning I just didn't feel like getting out of bed. I was thinking I would call in sick or something. My alarm kept ringing and I kept putting it on snooze, telling myself I would get up the next time it went off. I was about to put it on snooze yet again when my sister walked into my room and took my phone out of my hand.

"You need to get up."

"I don't want to. I really don't feel like."

"You have to go to work," she said in that motherly tone of hers.

I knew she was right but I really didn't want to. "Can't I just call in sick?"

"No. you're not calling in sick."

"Why? I'm sad. I just need to be in bed."

"Shut up and get out of bed. I will drop you to work."

"Fine," I said grumpily.

Fifteen minutes later she was back in my room.

"Ready?"

"Seriously... I just got out of the shower, give me ten minutes."

"Okay, I made you coffee. Do you want it now or should I mug it for you?"

"Mug it please."

About fifteen minutes later, we left. I decided it was a good thing I was going to work. That way I could concentrate on work, keep my mind busy and not think about him. I really hoped I could survive the day. When I reached my office, I quickly said goodbye to my sister and ran in because I was late.

Half an hour into the day, I seemed to be doing well, until Rohan messaged me. He didn't really say much; just a "Hey". I read it, but didn't respond. I just didn't know what to say. I went back to my work but couldn't concentrate much. Struggling with my thoughts for close to fifteen minutes, I went back to read that message. I still hadn't decided if I should reply or not. Finally around lunch time I wrote back, "Hey". I know it sounds stupid that I waited so long to say just that, but I didn't know what else to say.

"Where are you?" He asked.

"At office, where else would I be?" I responded, trying to sound normal.

"Uh huh," he wrote back.

I didn't respond first, then half an hour later I him a smiley face. I couldn't ignore him because I didn't know how to do that. He didn't reply and I went back to work.

Later that evening when I was home, I got a message from him again, "Where are you?" It made me laugh. I used to message him every single day when I was leaving work just to let him know.

I replied back, "Home".

"What're you doing?" He replied immediately.

"How does it matter?" I responded. I was still feeling a little hurt and irritated that he was being so normal like nothing had happened.

"So you're going to be like this now?" He asked.

"What do you want me to be like?"

"What's that supposed to mean?"

"You tell me you want to be friends. I'm trying. Now what more do you want from me?" I started crying again as I typed that.

"You're being mean now."

"I'm being mean? I fucking love you. You leave me and I'm being mean. Seriously!"

"I told you it's not about you. I do love you too."

When I read that, I wanted to throw my phone against the wall in frustration.

"If you really loved me, then you'd have been with me."

"It's not that simple."

"It is that simple, Rohan."

"I can't explain it. I just can't do this."

"And I can't be friends with you."

"Why?"

"Because I love you; and I can't just stop all of a sudden. What do think I am? I don't have some on-off switch for my emotions like you seem to have."

"That's not fair. It's not like that. I still do love you, but I just can't be in a serious relationship with you."

"I don't understand that."

"I'm not asking you to stop loving me."

"So what are you saying? You want me to love you and be friends with you at the same time? That's not possible."

"Then just be friends with me."

"I don't know, I just don't know anything right now."

"Okay."

I didn't respond; I put my phone away and went off to sleep. Four hours later, I woke up and thought about it all. I typed a reply to his message, "I can try the whole being friends' thing."

I was not sure if I could. I just didn't want to lose him. I wanted him in my life. Besides, before anything else we were friends.

SCATTERED THOUGHTS

My thoughts are scattered
My heart is all yours
My love is lost
As I lose a little part of use each day
My mind wanders
To times that used to be
To smiles
That weren't broken
To hearts
That were wild
To passion
That was so hot
It could put the best of lovers to shame
Now here we are
You smile at me
And I try to fight back the tears
I miss you needing me
I miss you wanting me
I miss the days you couldn't get enough of me
Now I watch as I lose
A little part of us each day
I wish to hold you in my arms a little longer
To kiss you till neither of us can breathe
While you try and forget me
I try and remember you
I know I should let go a little
But I don't know how
I'm tired of pretending
That this is easy
Because the truth is
I love you too much
To let this go
But I know I can't stay
It's so easy to say

I need to leave
It's easy to say
I need to let this go
But only I know
How difficult it is
To stop feeling the way I do
I miss you
You're special to me
You're my Rohan

THIS IS LOVE

It had been almost a month. We had barely spoken to each other. Initially we both tried to make it work and tried to be friends, but then it got complicated and confusing. He was so formal and distant or maybe I was. But after a while it began to feel like we were forcing ourselves to be friends. It felt rather pointless. I started to distance myself from him as much as I could. I began to avoid the places we both used to go to or had gone when we were together. I was just afraid to bump into him. I was not sure if I was ready to see him again.

In this one month, I had mastered the art of pretending to be fine, but only I knew the truth. Only I knew how I much I still loved him and how often he would cross my mind. I still felt the same way about him.

Then finally there came a day when I knew I had no choice and I would have to see him. It was Karan's birthday.

The funny thing was it felt like the first day I was meeting him. My heart was racing; I was really nervous. When I saw him, my heart stopped and came to a sudden halt. He gazed at me the way he had when we had first met. It felt magical, like it was meant to be this way. In that one moment, I knew I felt like nothing had changed.

"Hey," I said, feeling a little tongue-tied.

"Hi," he responded, still gazing at me, his eyes piercing through my heart.

I looked away. I was too afraid to feel the way I did. Should I give it one more shot and fight for him? Or should I continue to pretend I was okay and just walk away?

"Can we talk?" I blurted out seconds later, not knowing what

I was going to say or what I was thinking. I don't know what had come over me. I just could not let him walk away again.

"I can't do this being friends thing. I don't want to be without you, and when I'm around you, I can't pretend that I'm all okay with this. I'm not okay, Rohan. I'm just not okay." I said trying to control my feelings and trying not start crying there.

"I can't either," he said, as he took my hand in his.

I stared at him. I was a little taken a back. He looked and me and smiled and continued to talk.

"I can't be with you and not kiss you. I want you in my life. You're the one who actually got me over the most fucked up relationship in my life, and I can never thank you enough for that. Baby, I hope things always remain nice between us, and that I can always have you in my life because I will always want my baby to be with me, and always have you. I do love you and I wish you could see that."

I still kept staring at him, not knowing what to say. He looked at me as if he knew I needed some answers, and continued,

"I was just not ready for something serious. I need to sort myself out even now, but I need you too. I love you."

"I love you too," I said.

He held my hand tight and spoke, "I can't be in a serious relationship right now and I can't be friends and I can't let you go. I don't want to lose you. I don't know myself what to do."

"I'm right here; I'm not going anywhere, baby. I just need you to love me back," I said. I could feel my eyes fill up with tears.

"I do," he responded as I hugged him.

"So if I can't be in a relationship right now and I can't be friends, then what is this?" He asked me sounding slightly worried.

I smiled and said, "Love."

He kissed me gently and just held me in his arms for a while.

Dear Rohan,

I don't know what happens next. Where we will be? Or what new turn our lives will take? Life is too short to not take chances. I don't know what the future holds for us. But I know one thing for sure: you changed my life. You reminded me what love is like and that it still exists. You reminded me that love really does conquer all. I have seen it on TV and read it in books, but being with you, I experienced it too.

I don't care if you're not prince charming or if you're not perfect. Perfect is boring, anyway. Sometimes fights are good, sometimes messy is good. We complement each other and I think that is perfect enough.

I have always been happy, loving you and being with you. We are Rohan and Aleah. We will always be Rohan and Aleah. Every time either of us has ever thought we could do without the other or even considered it, the other one has pulled us back together. We fight but we always make up. We get jealous but we always make sure we understand each other's importance in our lives. We doubt at times, but we trust the love we share. There are times we both have thought that we have had enough and have even wanted to walk away, but we both know we can't stay away from each other. We always find a way to creep back into one another's lives. This is Love in its simplest form.

Love is simple. Love is when you kiss me out of the blue. Love is when you stay awake even though you are very tired and talk to me till I want you to. It's when you are at my door with a bag of potato chips just because I have a craving or when you lecture me a little about how I should take care of myself when I'm sick.

Love is when you are scared you will lose me to someone else but deep down inside you know I love you more than anything else. It's every time you know something is bothering me or something is on my mind without my saying a word. It's when you surprise me with the sweet thing you do, like the flowers which you got me out of the blue or going to the restaurant of my choice. By the way, I thought it was really sweet when you brought me your favourite flower because you didn't know my favourite.

It's in the way I irritate you so much that I know I'm testing your patience and you get irritated and still don't say much. We both know you still love me. It's the way we know each other a lot more than others do, or ever will maybe. The way you know when I'm crying on the phone and lying when I say I'm not.

Love is in that moment when I first kissed you. It's in the way I look into your eyes, shy and vulnerable; and all you do is hold me tight and make feel safe, like I am the only thing that matters to you. It is love when in the cold hours of the night I wear your clothes and they would keep me warm. It is love, the way my warm heart melts with you around. All these moments... that's what love is all about. It's the small things that count. It is the times you took care of me when I was sick or just went out of your way to make me feel comfortable. Those late night trips to in and out just because I was hungry and there wasn't anything to eat. You didn't have to go out of your way but you did because you cared about me. It's these tiny moments that build some of the strongest relationships.

You will never know what the future has in store for you. All we can do is just keep waiting for the right time for it all to work out. Who really knows?

What I do know is that in reality, fairy tales do exist. The only difference between Cinderella and her prince and us is that we have to make our own fairy tale come true.

I don't know if when you read this we will be together or not. But I do know that I will still love you. What I do know is that you will always be special to me. I know that we will still be friends because we promised each other that we would never let go of our friendship because more than anything else we were the best of friends. And maybe you will actually be sitting right next to me when you're old and wrinkly and reading this with me. If not, well I think this is still the most amazing love story and I will always remember it; remember you and remember our love.

Your little idiot
Aleah